kye

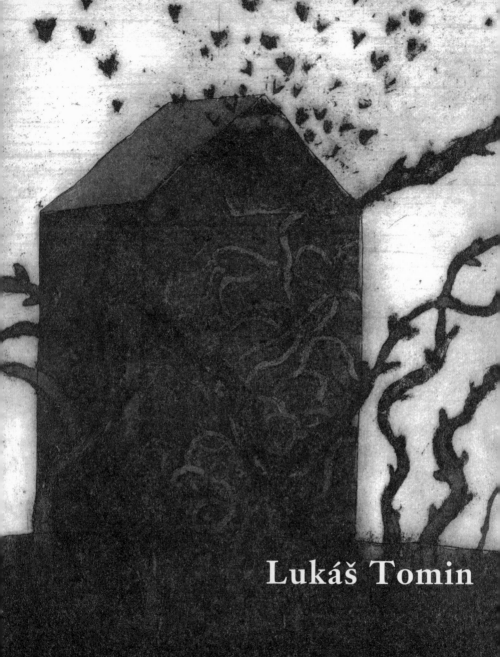

Lukáš Tomin

WITH ARTWORK BY
Alf Van der Plank

k y e

TWISTED SPOON PRESS

PRAGUE • 1997

ISBN 80-901257-8-6

part 1

Sitting suddenly in his chair. Blinding the pain felt so sub-limely just before. Totally out of the question this hungrying. I mean the holding of hands as the food is slipping by. I mean the shaking of feet as the stomach is holding tight. I mean the bug in the belly the bug in the lung the bug in the head. I mean the decomposing. I mean when two of us meet two of a kind we are singing. This dreaming of the two hands strapped together to supplicate. This weaving of the web.

Between my thighs I have an elastic cord and I feel sprightly. I Kye.

Together I and Kye and Lucy are beautiful in this world which is not of this world nor of the one after. Nor of the one between nor of the one inside. Where uneating with flat-tened stomachs we try to find softness. Where someone in sickness is stealing an apple. Where pomegranates. Wash your handkerchief in somebody's bloodwound. Where takers are catchers and catchers aren't takers. Where naked bones tear up the bed sheets.

Naked Kye.

There he was, discharged. Pen down. Free to sit anywhere you like. Even under the noses of the holy, free to sit, so that with upturned faces they may rape the sky. Troublesome shooter, Kye, aiming very high. Lucy shies away twitching a corner of her mouth. It is going to be a rainy winter. The poplar trees, with dreadful indolence, have decided to blossom. Last year's wine, long passed through bellies, impregnates. Cigarette butts once sucked. Staring through a dirty window at a glass stained with colour Kye wishes. A rabbit wishes, too, making it plain to the guinea. Pigs, too, want to live. Too? Yes, Key too wants to live, as through some grave he burrows. Lend me some space to live, he screams, and I shall never give it back. I'll put my bulk in it and I'll keep at it until it bursts. And the winter is going to be hard.

Do you know what is going to happen, my boy? You are going to have your pencil broken. Thus speaks precaution. Hospitals prove it. And cats bleeding in broken panes.

We are of course concerned with finding a path to truth. Therefore, Kye has constructed a fence. Birds, shitting merrily, squat there. And dogs, from piss-post to piss-post.

A bath, to clean his body, his soul hanging on a line to sunbleach. An envelope full of rags that do not need to be forgiven. An antelope buckling its way through studs of leather. A bishop, skirts up, singing in the rain. A tapestry, woven by maidens of promise, jerking in the wind. A coyote, befriended by Beuyes, reading the papers. And in Abney Park Cemetery a girl, face in palms, strolled softly through the wet-protecting earth.

What does a sky feel when you scrape it, Kye wondered, not scraping it, sitting in his chair, looking at the dirt, and beyond it, at himself, and beyond it, at the dark, and beyond it, the colour that had disappeared. And beyond it the nonsense that is viewed from the other side.

When Kye speaks the animals respond. The grass, bending over, listens. Only Man, the common denominator, writhes in pain and shouts, Bakshish! and he also shouts, God! and she also shouts, Man! and then Man, and woman, and man, shout, Bakshish!, and, Less! And then in unison they shout More! through Less! But the rabbit wishes for something else and shows it to the guinea pig.

In the mornings the prodigious courtyards. Walking through the gothic he leans against a buttress in the hope of supporting a wall. A postman, back crooked for the weight, brushes against uninvited hands. Clasp them in prayer and crawl on the knee-hollowed concrete.

I am Kye of the underbelly region. Snakes make their nests there, and lollipops. On a particularly fine day I can hear the bell strike a quarter of some hour. Today, throwing a lasso over a lamp, I strain to remember. A grandmother dying in an accident that I didn't see. For I wasn't there for I was out. A grandmother I loved who loved little green men who loved her. Who came to visit her at night to keep her company. To whom, despite the fact that she was a diabetic, I would bring bottles of sweet white wine grown on the hill above the river. It would not do her harm. Later, in an abandoned flat, a red-hot stove became her enemy. She fought with it and burnt the place down, narrowly escaping. But I didn't see it for I wasn't there. For I was out.

Out in the street Kye shivers, unable to take another step. Sweat, gluing his feet to the pavement and hands to a rubbery air. It is this place that reeks of being out of balance. I am not out of balance. He sits down on the pavement curb wishing he was in the water, wishing he was propped up. Gently carried, a new-born slipping out to swim, slipping out to float. Instead, the chest is making tractor shudder sounds. Attempting to stand up to go to the door to go to the bank to get some dosh. Wavering trembling is it cancer is it? Cancer = absence of will is it? To live is it? Little green men friends of a mad old woman indeed. And Lucy with her bad breath cotton wool in nostrils while doing it or else nose turned to window hoping for a whiff of air. Give me your hand, name-less one, nectar-tongued one, soft-skinned one, beloved.

To get some dosh hand inarticulate signing. Beads of sweat on forehead eyelids lowered. A junkie, the clerk whispers smiling under her whiskers to the left, and to the right. Dosh in, dosh out. To feed. Still wants to. Himself. Cancer = absence of will.

Life. A dustbin beckons, tear the asphalt off the street and in there with it. Then at least the stumbling over cobblestones. Then at least a reason. Then shoes in cracks and the falling down of laughter.

Irish cheddar cheese and two white rolls and butter. And the old crumbs swept off and new ones to deposit. And an old newspaper to sit on and a new newspaper to read. And a box to switch on and a wall to lean against and a moron to — wink at?

Sitting in a green crown of a tall tree. Holding you by the slimmest of waists, my eternal one. Holding you up like that, to frighten you a little, in the air, just softly, between the tips of my fingers. And you, looking at me, purring, knowing that I will never, never, drop you.

Perhaps I could slither sideways, an own-invented horizontal-mobile mammal. That way, the full-frontal impact eliminated, the onward-rushing breaking over the sharpness of the eye's corner. But what if a change of direction is required, a crossing of a street?

An ugly maggot feeds on my breast, she says, but you can't see it. It's an ugly maggot that you can't see. Kye, hovering between heaven and earth, dropped her.

My head is a gas-filled balloon. My feet, heavy anchors, smash against too-sharp roof-tops. When having landed having to balance on two five centimeters in diameter stumps. Is there nobody out there to find my biker's boots? She was pretty there, lying squashed on the ground, maggot-less. Her hair spread out nicely round her head. Intact, the head. Smile on the lips. Eyes open. Your breasts will never, ever feed a maggot again, my beloved, my darling.

You'd get run over by a car, of course, slithering sideways across a street. No stopping the onward-rushing from the back, non-created bipod.

It is all as it should be, the cars and the fumes and the no time. And the too much of it. Plodding through bodies on their way to. On their no way. Kye is as he should be, head scarf or no, eye scarf for pirate, a cheek scar. Shoulders swept forward, sea-wide legs, prowling grin on face. Totally BALANCED. A dagger blue-tacked on belt, secure. Chest as broad and solid as the Wall of Hunger. Golem-like lightness.

Shivering in a corner. Blasting the mind with the prospect of — supermarket cheaperness. Afraid to take another step. Afraid to stand up, even, for fear of — keeling over. Ships, waves, waters and boats, weightward. Paint and grease in the hair, old make-up, Jack. Jack who is a girl, Jack who doesn't care. Jack who is beautiful. Jack who works with Kye in a corner shivering. Jack who says no. To Henry Miller and Hemingway she says no. For POLITICAL reasons. Jack who hasn't read Henry Miller or Hemingway. Jack who says no. Jack washed. Once a week unsmelly Jack. Jack in black. Jack who loves Eire and Kye who loves it. Jack who has been and Kye who hasn't. Primary feelings, robots on longlegs. Tarbabies. Piss in the sink to avoid putting the toilet seat up and down. As courtesy to the opposite sex. A coin? Sundance in the rain and raindance in the sun. Let the heritage of England bloom. Poisonous daffodils, let us celebrate the rites of spring.

Yes, the winter is going to be hard. For the spring to come the winter must be hard. Look at me, the sweat on my palms beginning to freeze. As I caress my hair, droplets turn to ice, like ornaments of a goddess. Kye is not alone, Kye has a goddess to think about and ornaments bestowed. Round every corner, today, some she resembles. A toe or a chin, resembles. A left nostril, a wrinkle on a right eyelid. A stray hair, like hers, falls over the bridge of a foreign nose. Her knee-cap artlessly glued to a clumsy joint. Her socket, filled with another's expressionless vileness. Her footsteps, her sounds, stuck on some hurrying heap of health.

Do I protest enough?

The streets are getting darker, he noticed, crawling now, still noticing, though through a distant echo. The shortest way to nigh, friend, is through the gutter, the gutter, the gutter. His body is singing, is singing, is singing. Stop. Somebody's calling. Ahoy there, buster, you motherfucker of an angel, it is not here, it is not here, it is not here. Hear me, flies in some swamp I dare not visit. When I extend my hand,

BITE IT! When I open my mouth, fill it. When I take off my pants, turn my tool into a workshop. Kye, awesome Kye.

The streets were getting darker. When I extend my hand, kiss it. Please, kiss it. Down in the dungeons they are trying to fill a void.

Never has a poet's love gone further, behind closed doors. In spaces minute, in spaces, large. Standing up, sitting down, lying down, on all fours. On the back, on the belly. Trapped. Hidden from the multitudes, I cover my face with shame. With my sticky, grey, jelly-like shame. Whereby I progress. Whereby I reach. Always, nearly always, I reach. In my trap in my freedom in my hut in my cell. In my virgin. Secular thoughts banished I contemplate, Thy womb. In my virgin. In my brainstorm. In my deadness. In my hunger.

A painting of a scream a scream of a friend a friend I have lost a blood-red sauce and a French-salad-dressing some poorly clad monster of a child rising up from the dirt from the depths of a dirt to punish to unsee to undo to catch by the balls to wring to smile to grin to laugh where have I been closed doors wanker eat madmen at funfairs heaven knows carry me touch me softly. Boil the bones to protect the flesh embalm it strip it cut it up French-salad-dress-it. Tumble beneath the weak lid slip in it swim in it. Lick it up.

Oh, I have seen it all.

Do I protest enough?

Doors closed.

Oh and when I fly, Mother of Invention, on wings of

plywood in the form of crosses attached to my wrists.

Oh and when I cry, swallowing Dead Seas.

Oh and when I.

Trois jeunes tambours, with me the jeunest. The evening is mild, unraining. La bouche en rose. The princess, in the window, fair. The breeze, mild, from the south. The king, old, ready to die. The ship, rich, ready to sail. The castle, crumbling, ready to fall. My charger, muzzle to moon, mane to the sea.

Suffusion. Salo. Salpetre. Sardonique. Sojourn. In this city of cold rails. In this labyrinth of worms. In this triangle of corpses. And with rosy lips she dropped the flower into his. His medallion of honour shone. Du jeunissime. Hurrah they shouted by the ship. Hurrah they shouted as they christened the ship. As they christened him. As they christened him the heir of boats. The fattened boat. The ship. The young heir to the boat. The screaming vessel. The organic watership. The cannons. The organic fire. In the bellies. Slime into barrels. Roll down Upper Street. Slime on the street. Fair princess. Rose en bouche. Capitulation.

And he wandered like a beggar from hand to hand.

Give me a rope to hold on to, a horizontal rope, stretching from north to south. Not from west to east or from east to west. Not a hand that sweats nor a hand that pulls up nor a hand that pulls down. Nor a hand that swings. I want a rope from north to south supported precisely by vertical compasses. The beer in this café costs much and tastes. In this

café that is not a café. Not in any metaphysical sense it is not a café. It is simply not a café which pretends to be a café. It is a non place. It is not a shit place. It is a non place. A shit place stinks. Of shit. Don't call a place a shit place if it does not stink of shit. The beers are the vertical compasses that support the horizontal rope that I must hold on to. They cost much.

Shut up, she bellowed, shut up, shut up, shut up.

They cost much.

Mischievously, like a little clown, like the little brat that comes in the shop to stick chewing gum on the books, he stuck a chewing gum on her thigh. What's that, she shouted, shut up, shut up, shut up, what's that. I stuck a chewing gum on your thigh, I stuck a chewing gum on your thigh, cunt. Shut up, shut up. Be with me, hold me, love me. Have my baby. Make us a cup of coffee. Three and a half sugars. Licorice. Cocoa. Milk it, milk the baby. The brat that sticks gum on the books, milk it. Callanetics. Amenities. I am afraid you've got the wrong address.

He sent him a postcard from Marseilles, from south to north.

Caroline, oh my English Caroline who wouldn't without a gum, must we always describe circles?

The darker the streets got the lighter his step became. Am I measuring time?

Immortally she took him in the morn and in the after and in the dusk and in what follows. Child of the sun. On the run.

She has been knowing the necessity of return.

Toss a flask in the sea.

Waves, clashing against imperial pages.

Bloodhounds.

Cigarette boxes.

As Kye rises from the pavement heart not beating fast nor thundering but simmering. On the pavement in the slime do I have to grovel? The necessity of return? Shut up, shut up, shut up? Beat me to it. As in the non-place he goes, beat him to it, knock over the bottles, smash the compasses, cut the rope. From north to south indeed he would want. What's that.

As blazing as hell the two feet that between them rattle a chain. Blazing with red paint and the rattle the crackle of plastic beauty-curls joined together. Ah oui, la deuxième sensation du roi pourri. Ah what next my lover a spear up my bum? Il faut pas s'ennerver.

A hair burns. While others work a hair burns and Paola awaits. Her burning teddy bear.

Paola is a bitter-sweet twenty-five-year-old Italian chicoletta. She has brown eyes and black hair and olive skin. She wants to be a singer. She likes hard boiled eggs because of salmonella. She likes spinach. She likes mozzarella. She crosses frontiers of vision. She crosses her legs. In black and white stripes. She is a predator. In black and white stripes. She paints walls. She moves. She's on the move from flat to flat. She has a cousin called Valentino. She's not a bad sort.

Oh my beloved, hiding beneath a bridge above a dirty river filled with mirrors.

And the arrow pierces my warriors breast.

You are a long time in coming back, engaged as you are in contemplating your miraculous features. Hall of Wisdom, Flower of Chastity, Lasko. Tremble, as I prepare a cocktail of deadly poisons. Lasko. On rocks sharper than your bones. Licking the salt off the seven seas. Pilgrim. Where I go nothing speeds up and nothing slows down, and nothing goes forward and nothing returns. It's like a bog without the necessary shit, past or present or potential. My trampled upon darling. Light a cigarette, squeeze it between the gums of your toothless mouth, and wash your knickers bare-bummed. My old darling. In the Paris of our dreams. Off with your tee shirt show me your dried-up tits. My beautiful lover. In the power of our dreams show them to me. Lasko. In the metanoia. Where you and I in towers of metal had held hands. Had trembled. Drink.

Kye had risen from the pavement. He made his way to a nineteen-years-old sickness. Had added his own. Sitting in your lap makes me feel younger, honey. Makes me feel. Risen. My trampoline. My spring-board. Sitting in her lap she made him feel younger, honey. Made him feel. When he couldn't dream. So on and on, mistaking a button for a nipple. Sleep naked beside me, I shall not fuck you, I shall touch you softly. Soberly, I shall tell you stories. Of past heroics. Of countries conquered. Of volcanoes embracing.

Of middle-men dead. Of traversing dark corners, of switching off lights, of daylight. He told her all this and he could
tell her more, but the sick child was drowsing. Head on the
counter cool on the forehead smoke in the nostrils. Bitten off
nails swimming in soup bowls. Prodigies. Televised encoun-
ters. Markets. The sick child is drowsing. Off, off to the.
Through puddles we approach, through mud-baths we enter.
We, giants of promise. Hold the door open for another
young lady of uncertain beginnings. Thighs, meditatively lax,
disjointed from the hips. I Kye you? She holds him tight, she
holds him tight not to fall over. Je vous demande pardon,
monsieur, he would like to hear her say in French, but
instead she blushes and grins, disjointed the blush and the
grin, and disappears in a crowd of safe-bets. Les bêtes m'ont
toujours été sympatiques.

It is the hour of my need. Where hills grow.

Suddenly, searching for a snowball in the sand. Hot, the
weather.

Kye smiled wryly.

The nonchalance.

Of it.

In the meadows where napkins settle like butterflies.

On the carpet.

Search me stranger.

Tomorrow is another day.

In truth.

In.

Winking at another he saw the morn coming.

Of a habit.

So this is the way things turn out to be in passion.

Of a habit.

Sing a song sing along to.

My way of describing.

Have you ever.

Experienced.

Trashy the way she stands.

Of acquiring to.

Tomorrow is today, baby, spread out.

Propositions.

Unacquired.

Lumps.

Unswallowed.

Throats.

Romantic sailors earthbound.

Crying.

For flying.

Fish out of water.

In truth.

Are dying.

Of a habit.

In perpetual silence the rustling of.

Sing along to.

Where one is the other is bound to.

Drop.

Of a tear so sweet on her cheek so salty to.
Dispose of.
Let run through the make-up on the necklace to.
Glitter.
Two bulging forward and a hole.
With an ending.
Try to be homeward try to be sane.
In the river.
Of your choosing.
Secure the wranglings of madmen.
On the beat.
To a nowhere.
Drastically diminished reach up for the apple.
To find it.
All rotten.
When in with the crowd out on your feet with a pearl.
To hunt for.
Send a love charm.
Send a letter.
To be cherished.
By a loner.
In a cavern.
Full of magic.
As we planned it.
Of a sadness.
Of a winter.
Shropshire druid.

Today of all days, thought Kye, should be my last. What with the zebra crossing yellow balls all broken. What with the trembling never stopping. What with the bread going stale. What with a lover long dead that memories can't resurrect. What with a wet matchbox.

Somewhere along the lyricism of wet slime. She appeared. Lucy.

Wet street. The street was wet because the winter was going to be hard. Des passagers tardifs. We are.

Listen, John, as I speak to you over this bottle. Listen. Drops are falling on a roof above our heads, listen, John. As I suck some blood from my thumb that I hurt as I listen. Or is it cats, John? On this roof that you didn't put there and I didn't. Have a drink, John, and tell me about your life.

Back on the trail of a hunted loved one, neck-deep in snow. Invisible leopards, leadless, lead me on. As I pour myself another to calm my liver. In this joint where sorrow is dispersed, in this joint where nobody shakes hands, in this joint where you and I, John, try to listen. To aquamarine blues.

Powerless and fragile my lover sits perched on a swan. She winks, now with her left eye, now with her right, at passing fish. I am not a fish. I am a sensational gold digger, away from fresh water, away from seas, making my way through Alaskan ice. I am a Red Indian, too. And when you speak, John, gun in readiness in holster, open fist on butt. I respect you, John, friend, as you squirt colour on the canvas I hold stretched out. On the canvas I pleated for you to squirt on. For you to embalm yourself in. Friend. And I cry for mummy, and mummy has gone for a walk. Not on the wild side. My lover is strangling the swan, now with her left eye, now with her right. She's neat. She drinks soda. She is. Developed. It is the transits that worry me. From lorry to lorry. Of merchandise.

Sleep, my beloved. Sleep. It isn't the time of day, to be awake. To dream awake. It isn't the time of year. Sleep, like the river, sometimes, sleeps, when the time, isn't, right. To be awake, honey. Do not search with your little finger the happiness you desire so terribly. Now. When everything is tense like an overtuned E and hollow. Come to a cave. A hollow. When this passes then I with a kiss will. Part your lips. But for now as good as dead sleep. In this greyness I must walk tumbling over twigs of wire. For now. For now trying to shake hands unworthy of touch. For now smiling at faces in crooked corners. In crooked pus-filled corners of eyes.

And to cross again the zebra crossing to the no-bar. Just about crossing it, with balance knocked off. With the smoke from the cigarette in the lungs knocking it off, triggering the fear. With the fear grown bigger with the sleep. With the sleep from last night sprawling all over me, hombre, the shadow. With the heart beating for the lungs and the lungs shaking for the heart. With the crossing of it.

And on the other side dressed-up dolls, with slitless wood in there in between. And I keep my cough inside my lungs and it shakes them, and knocks off the balance. And I would like to cough if the fear hadn't got bigger. Of spitting it all out. Because still life after all what's this. But still life. But still, life. Perhaps one day still.   , still. The gun in the holster I will not ask you to use it, John. Because you know after all. Or not that much. Aye, not that much. Aye this wooden thigh of this wooden doll that when licked doesn't glisten. Doesn't tighten. Doesn't spread. It is raining. Outside, the road, is wet. The pavement, too, is wet. And coats. When I want a beer I ask for one. This is what Kye asks for, a beer. And an ashtray to flick ash into. And a stool I ask for when a stool is between two people who are asking each other things. I ask for this stool saying excuse me is this stool free and they say yes. Or one of them says this. They are happy I ask for the stool because they put the stool there to separate the asking from the saying. I move the stool away and I sit on the stool and I hear the silence and then I hear the saying. Of small things I hear it, the saying, and the wood turns into flesh and glistens. And I sit on the stool and when I want a beer I ask for it. And then the no-bar turns into a bar. And then the shaking of the lungs stops. And then the heart I stop to hear. And then the rain outside stops. And then the cars outside drive into the sun into Europe. And then my beloved sits in the palm of my hand and tells me stories. And she bathes in the river an unpolluted river she bathes in. Naked she bathes in it and she tells me stories as she floats in it. Because this is the way with beloveds. And I sit in the garden

and watch her do it. I sit on the stool in the bar in the garden and watch her. Because when she does it she is beautiful. And even if she doesn't do it and just floats. And I sit here and I don't feel sorry for myself and I float in something, too. Like that postcard you'd shown me, John, of somebody afloating. Of somebody afloating on a belly I don't have. More like a dried-up skeleton afloating on the river of her dreams, John. Like a fossil, John. Like charcoal, John. On the river of my dreams of her dreams, John.

The caress of a cockroach in an old boot. Is that life?

Presently, Kye, in a contemplation of growth, has stopped talking to John.

Presently, naked, he ponders.

The inevitable.

Where the inevitable is a succession of evitables.

That is what he, presently, Kye, ponders.

Like a cockroach in an old boot.

Like a madman in a barn rotting in the stench of his making.

In small dark places.

Where loneliness is great and undisturbed.

Like a map of a large country impossible to visit.

Of a great and large country.

Of America.

With a beloved.

Kye is now pondering impossibles.

Compounded by possible possibles.

That is the state of mind Kye is in now.

Parisless and Americaless.

Flightless.

And as he sits there naked he extends his empty hand into the air.

And then he lets it fall.

This, he thinks, is the destiny of someone crouched in a box.

In a small dark space.

With no holes to look through out.

With not a sweeping gesture to go by.

With rabbit-like persistence in hide-outs.

Like glued to the inside of a tambourine.

Without the deep echo of a bass drum.

With only the rattle of metal and the tin sound of the skin.

Unlike the baroque expansion he will know later. Unlike the arching of backs in extasies of passion. Unlike the flowing of juices the screaming of pain the howling of pleasure the swimming the running the voluptuous resting. Unlike the cutting of wood with great sweeping movements, unlike the axe bringing down the sun.

That is something to hope for, said Kye, as he raised his hand. And then let it fall down again. I shall go hunting, then, desiring blood. Bur for now, John, friend, admirer of my pallor, you must listen to a screeching sound emanating from a hole in my heart. For that is the way with loveless beloveds. Screeching in dust covered hovels. Cocks half-filled with frustration. Sniffing unerotic sweat. Own sweat, unmingled. Only from time to time sniffing equally unerotic sweats of equally unmingled Jacks. In London town. In London, England. In a dust covered hovel. Where sharks bite without teeth, inflicting blunt injuries. Sharks swimming in dusts.

I love you.

I love you he said to the tree from which she had hung clinging to his little finger. For he now travelled through nature-filled lands.

Parks. Sitting in a park with a bottle in a hope. Difficult to sit in a hope with a bottle in a park. Alone in a. Now if with a partner but then this a matter for another contemplation. For a conglomeration. Yes, of two or three. But one alone in a park with a bottle is not a conglomeration of elements of the same species that most certainly it is not. And with a hope. For as the bell rings the cat prowls awkwardly round table legs mimicking the tiger. The cat in my head. The cat who says to me in my head: This is a time for hope. But you are awkward, I say to it, mimicking the tiger.

And so, John, you need a vision.

Kye walked in the rain. Spastics, standing in fixed spots, wrists tied to lampposts, waved to him. Tied to the necks of the lamps of the lampposts, the wrists, with nylon strings. Obeying the wind. The wind therefore beckoning to Kye. But can I respond, feet stuck to the pavement, torso vertiginously somewhere between the street and the sky? Ha, wind?

And yet there were times when these things were possible, when flying over oceans was as easy as pursing his lips to whistle. When there were caves in which to hide, and plants on which to feed. When birds sang. When shit smelled sweet and piss was holy water watering the holy ground. When drops of sweat from the armpits turned into pearls of meaning. When grease in the hair became Magdalene's oils. And Judas' coins didn't betray. And we were about to die.

And Kye was walking in the rain.

In the dead of night.

In the dead of night past eleven in London town.

No more beers to be had, no more compasses or directions or buzolas. Just there one foot in front of the other carefully to place. Too late now to even buy Raider or Rustler. Regretting that. At least open cunts to look at. At least pictured ways.

And in the rain he said to John: Come, let us follow our instincts.

But in London town past eleven instincts are dead.

If we were in Paris past eleven, John, I would say to you: Come, let us follow our instincts. Instead, now, let us place one foot carefully in front of the other, like blind men. Like blind men with a mission. Give me a cigarette. I reach in my pocket and give myself one. I light it. Don't worry, John, I am used to fending for myself. Talk to me.

I am John your best friend. I walk with you in the rain. I am Dutch.

Yes, John, you are, you are.

I place one foot carefully in front of the other, just as you tell me to.

You are a pal, friend, stop in your tracks. I embrace you in the name of something more than brotherly and less than you know what. As water trickles through my fingers clasped behind your back. Talk to me.

—

Lost for words, hombre, amigo? No wonder, no wonder, the closeness of it all, eh?, the emotion. It's like a great combustion of ideas not wanting to bust, eh? Am I right? Or is it just a spasm of directions uncertain? Ha? Never mind, never mind. Just hold my hand like something more than a brother and less than you know who. I won't hold it against you, your silence. It's just that I am like a voiture en panne, you see. In need of a rope. Don't be afraid to hold me by the hand, for Christ's sake, your sweat will mingle with the rain. Shoulders thrown back we advance, heroes of the night. You and I, John, friends, supporting one another.

Holding on to each other with frog-like hands. Comme des crapauds noircis glistening in the dark. Your tall big body and my thin tall body. Our legs entwined with a hint of sex. With a hint of sex we both detest. Haemorrhaging from the arse we both envisage. Give me a cigarette, bend over to get it, from the inside of your sock, where you keep them dry, don't touch me, light it. Your arse is big, that much I've noticed. Maybe the hole in your arse is big, too, that much I have not been able to notice, yet. And won't try to notice and won't try to see it. And won't try to fill it. But you madden me, brother of my soul, with your big hands. And with your big mouth. I was handcuffed once to a table leg and a big guy was kicking me in the balls. He had a big mouth. He had stone blue small eyes. He had a beard. Not like you who don't have a beard. Who don't have stone blue small eyes. You aren't vicious enough, loverboy, John, pest. He was vicious, that other boy, that stone-eyed one. He had a medal, too. Had a gun. But his eyes were small, you see, not like yours. The corners of his mouth were sharp, pointed downwards, made engravings, in his flesh. Unlike your blunted edges. When he smiled the grimace on his face was. Was. Lion-like? But he never smiled. He was like your average sailor, really, John, except for those eyes. You have sailor's eyes, I think, John. Wide and broad and seeing, horizons reflecting. Gentle. Though I think perhaps sailors were not so gentle. I mean perhaps they were sharp exactly I mean limestone tool sharp and all that could do you harm you know. Could tie you by the ankle to a table and by the wrist to a kitchen sink and I mean hey. But you are not at all like those sailors, John. I mean I suppose those sailors had blue eyes like some blue stones, right. And I mean you don't have blue stones. But I mean I don't think those sailors were gentle. Not a bit. A lot of rum I mean they drank those sailors. Doesn't make you gentle, that rum. What they did with those women they did like they did it with those boys.

Couldn't keep it up otherwise couldn't keep it thick you know I mean. John. You aren't mean at all, John, you aren't, honest. That other boy was mean, that other boy with stone blue eyes was, honest. When he kicked me in my fragility he was, honest. He was honest. Twenty-five maybe with a beard he was, the rascal. He was sharp, John, not like you. His fingernails were polished.

The clock struck ten. Somewhere on the horizon it struck it, ten strokes some time in the day or in the night, the dirt on the window, the school building glued to the wall of the backyard, the dirt on the tree in the yard, contributing to the uncertainty. Kye rubbed his eyes in an orthodox manner, felt the cavity below his rib cage. All in all, no surprises this morning or this evening as it might be. Place stinking of dog piss and fresh paint. Beer spilt on floor. Half a bottle of a half a bottle of scotch under the desk. Socks, dirty and clean mingled, scattered, waiting to be sniffed to determine. Similar with other articles of assorted clothing. All in all, the physicality of it all reassuring. Propped on his elbows, Kye contemplated pulling up his knees. Head heavy dangled on his neck, puppet-like. The effort of the pulling up of the knees unattempted. Head heavy disjointed from spine fell back on the pillow. Spine followed rejoining. Arms limp alongside the body. Try shifting the left arm to the edge of the mattress, finger by finger. Feel the steel or is it a plastic string? The fifteen centimeters of air between dirt and the soft of your palm. Then feel the soft of the ash on the hard of the wood. Then put the right foot over the left foot like a heavy hot body of a bullring bull. Then edge slowly the left hip, millimeter by millimeter, towards the wall, thus lifting the right hip. Now, lying on your left side, you have a horizontal perspective of things. Haphazard objects normally worn or used mindlessly by the adult homo assume gigantic and threatening proportions. Particularly as you have lost perception of the rest of your physiognomy. Only the eyes remain, and a cerveau lourd that pins them to the pillow. Eyes on strings of inner phlegm. Eyes on top of one another, the right pressing on the left. A shoe, gaping, swallows an empty matchbox. A needle, stuck in a floorboard, a heroic gesture of a warrior prince. Demanding entrance, requiring confrontation. In an abstract way, for no specific reason. And the prince has left it there, an eternal vibrating thrust of defiance. And I salute the prince, and my limbs begin to give a sign of life. And my penis stiffens. I see a girl in bondage inside the castle. Her arms spread her wrists chained to hooks in the wall. The place is wet and cold and dark. Two Easter candles on either side of her, flames licking tongues warming her flanks. She is shivering, nipples erect, exposed clitoris moist. Round each ankle a viper waiting for the slightest movement of her feet to attack. From time to time she moans, turning her head from side to side. Her eyes, fixed uncertainly to a point in the shadows of the ceiling. The prince, sitting on a stone slab in the middle of the room, watches. He approaches her and, gently, places a python round her delicate neck.

If he could stop this trembling. If he could reach inside his lungs and take it, this trembling, like a ball of astral dust, and push it out, and hold it, at arms length, and examine it, and drop it, and let it free. The particles dispersing in other tremblings of other trembling men, perhaps somewhere creating some solidity. But, for now, the bottle to lips, yet again, only to calm it. For the strength of reaching and pushing out of anything has been left somewhere on the right bank of the Seine. With the beloved boatwrecked, skull splintered on an ancient stone. With a broken string. With a drunk at Le Mazet who'd played with David Byrne. With a cat on a roof. With a sick dog. With a blonde of wooden receivings. With a mother who wished her mother dead. With a daughter of elephant thighs. With bad breath. With a once-upon-a-time beauty with a whip-lashed arse. With a sick dog. With a child on a roof about to jump. With a fearless dove. With a broken promise. With me. Kye looked up and observed the spider eating the wasp, carefully avoiding its sting.

Le bâton rouge

Serves as punishment

As an erotic device

As a symbol of openings

As a pilgrim's staff. It is my guide and mentor. I use it to fly over rocks. It uses me. When I propel my bloodstream.

There are tombs to see in Egypt.

You go there once, you go there twice, like a drunkard swaying on an olive branch.

You are a happy man.

That way.

And when the sun goes down at five in the afternoon.

You are.

Ready.

All this is just a question of practice.

Tomb-going.

With a red whip.

Succulent passions overwhelm the heart as it strives to grab hold of a hip-line.

Today and tomorrow and a little bit later.

Sweetest honey.

When I grab hold of a hip-line.

Surrender to the sailor.

And everything will be nice and quiet. And the seas will be far away, deep inside his breast. And the bees will hum there gently, protected from the winter frosts. And you will have strangled the gulls.

Kye, high above the level of the water in the gutter, winked at a passing swallow. She hadn't made it back to the warmth, either. She had a hard time of it, too. She had kids, elsewhere. He had kids, nowhere. She was going to die, somewhere in a bush, in a park. He was going to, get drunk.

The clock on the horizon struck ten. A stagnating clock in a city where taking a step amounts to standing still. The dirt on the tree, however, increased. The contents of the bottle showed a private retrogression of time. All is well.

And then the lamp began to flicker.

And in the flickering I saw a face.

And in the face an ant hid, gnawing at the underskin.

It was a face I knew.

But it was a face I did not recognize.

I crawled on that pavement, ploughing saliva and dogshit. With my bare knuckles and with my soon-to-be-bare elbows I crawled on that pavement. Ploughing under-snort and undershit. Chinbone exposed I hurt many a toe. Many a delicate toe, I hurt. Delicate toes like my baby's I hurt crawling on that pavement I hurt I hurt. Hey, hey, hey. Wanna hot dog? Hot shit. Then I sort of propped myself up I sort of propped myself up to speak. Hey, hey, hey. Wanna hot shit. And I sort of crawled there on this pavement sort of propping myself up. Wanna hot shit. With a stiletto heel in my ear wanna hot dog. You were a beauty, baby, in your day-time. In your nighttime you were a louse, yeah, wanna hot dog. I hurt your toes, baby, with my sharpness. Gee gee the rats in the sewers I can see them in the gutters. I can smell them in the gutters. Like your delicate toes. To left and right, discarded pornshots. Like your delicate toes. Give me a breakie, like you give it left and right. Ecrasée sur ma paume. On all fours with pants down let me find refuge, sweetly.

Kye remembered eating oranges, sweet oranges from Cuba, full of pips. It was there that his grandmother died, near the market where Kye bought sweet oranges from Cuba. And the little green men went to sleep. Under the truck. He didn't like these oranges, they were full of pips, they were too sweet, and the skin was too thin and difficult to peel. He preferred watermelons, but there were no watermelons in winter. He liked peaches, too, and cherries he picked from trees in the summer and plums he picked from trees in the autumn. He had been a physical sort of kid.

It would be nice to have a telephone and he would pick it up and friends would phone. He had had a telephone and he would pick it up and there would be friends phoning. Hi Kye, they would say, and he would say, Hi. There was always something happening and so they would arrange to meet and do something. There was always something exciting happening and there was always danger and there was always fun. There was always fun in the danger and when even smaller in the winter when there was snow they would cover their steps by trailing fir-tree branches behind them tied to their waists by a piece of washline. They did this in the remote regions of public parks, not in the streets, they were no fools and they knew that with so many footsteps already printed on the pavement theirs would not be visible, or even better, their pursuers would get confused and fall under a tram or under a bus or under a taxi or under a police car and with a bit of luck not under an ordinary car as they didn't want the driver to get into trouble. And so anyway then they would part and then they would give one another a ring again when they got home to arrange another meeting for the next day or for the day after next at the latest. Or just before they would part they would see another friend coming down the street an older friend with licence to roam late into the evening and then he would pursuade them to go with him to Malá Strana to look at the ghosts. And although they would get hell for it later they would go with him just for the fun of the danger of it. And then at the end of the evening they would ask him to phone them but he was an older friend and they would have to phone him to arrange a meeting to which he would never come because he was an older friend. But they phoned one another when they got home. Later they phoned girls, and girls phoned them.

Later, Kye thought. Later in cafés in a torn winter coat with different friends and with danger and with fun not in the danger. He wanted to spit a pip from a Cuban orange through his teeth.

The lamp stopped flickering and the face he knew but could not recognize was gone.

There was a perfume she wore that I loved. I can't remember the name of it.

Up on the roof pigeons play dirty games.

Up on the roof we'd played dirty games.

In the blood-stained robes of angels.

Wrapped in damp white sheets we tried to keep warm. In the attic, underneath the heavy beams that seemed to be the true foundations of the house. We played like that, shivering from cold which gave us a sense of reality. Or with bare bellies on the stone cold floor. Or touching the cold-sweating walls. Or standing on the terrace in the rain. Or touching.

In my old age I get sentimental, thought Kye, kneeling on the bed, head between knees propping himself up on it to squeeze the hands underneath the shoulders to lift himself up to go to piss. Necessary to put on shoes. If not, necessary later to go back to the bathroom with shoes in hand to wash the filth from the floor from the feet. Careful not to touch the floor he drew his pair of imitation converse basketball trainers to the edge of the mattress, put them on, stood up, and went to the john.

John, my friend, I think of you as I try to piss in the American way. It's the only way to piss, I think, for me, right now. I am in need of BIG spaces and BIG thoughts. This water closet has charm. The walls are soaked through from burst pipes. There is about a centimeter of pure Chalk Farm water on the lino. In it swim half-dissolved sheets of toilet paper, tampons, a woman's breast and the letters »EVIL RICH«. On the bottom of the deluge, two nails lie heavily. The dimensions of the place are about one by one and a half meters. You can use the bath, there is a bath, if you want to, which is not very often. We shall make the place look groovy when another John who can do anything and who understands motorcars and who lives here gets down to it.

It was nice.

But it was not big, despite Kye calling the loo the john. And big thoughts didn't come to him, only small trembling ones like plankton about to be swallowed by a whale. Or a passer-by about to be crushed by the World Trade Center. By an infinite succession of silent glass plains. By a shadow.

I hear tigers instead of wolves roam the remotest regions of eastern Slovakia. It is a fact of singular political importance. The levels of state deer are insufficient to feed them. The Prague Zoo is overcrowded. However, heroes can always be found.

WHAT in the name of God am I doing in the sun?

It is the new migration of nations.

To drink beer by the gallon is no longer possible.

I would like to have a prize presented to me.

I would like to have a telephone.

Yesterday, someone jumped from the top of Notre-Dame, killing a teenage girl on impact.

The Russians are great.

The Catholic Church.

Yesterday, someone's torn-off foot killed a baby in a cradle on impact.

It is still possible to drink beer by the can.

Or by the bottle.

Yesterday, Passion was launched.

Can you read the signs of our times, John? Is there a corner of the Earth where the red squirrel has not been eliminated by the black? Where the few bears left do not feed on rubbish dumps? Where you can hear the roar of a lion without the roar of a jeep? Or a worse?

But the day outside was too heavy and the din in the

chest too loud to pursue long lost figures of thought. Kye, like a dog beaten too long and too consistently, kept close to the fences of front gardens.

Somewhere, some time, he had dreamed about a garden underneath a rock by the sea where they would both hide, playing. Before he dropped her from the tree to get rid of the maggot. Before the trembling.

The train that was taking him to work could should be taking him away from here. But the train was a little train with a limited distance span. But it had the charm of a pretended Romanov returning from an afternoon spent at Kew with two crusts of bread and a bottle of East German sekt. Or perhaps the Romanov was not pretending but still had eaten two crusts of bread and drunk a bottle of East German sekt. There was no Romanov, however, on the 12:45.

It is a curious thing that when you can hardly crawl you buy a pair of fancy boots and shoe polish. Is it a sign of hope for better times to come or is it a preparation for the lying in state? Or is the lying in state a better time? Is it perhaps the hope of restoring the maggot?

Kye, in his new fancy boots, measured Upper Street from Highbury Corner to the King's Head. The Union Chapel, still echoing with Steve Reich's xylophones. The Town Hall, with twenty-five thousand unemployed hanging from it. The pub finally, with theatre lights extinguished, with lunch just being cooked, with a couple of drunks at the bar, with a couple of drinks to be poured. And when the sweating stops, and when the shoulders become proud, it is time to knock the dust off books.

Haila was a lovely, hysterical, screwed-up, big daughter of Poles. As ugly as Wroclaw, she didn't know the language. Elegance personified, she knew her Figures. She had a giraffe's neck, a zebra's bum, a horse's thighs, a pig's calves. She loved to talk, very loudly, provoking disgusting grimaces, she wanted to provoke charmed smiles. She loved to talk about personal things, about her calves, her thighs, her neck and the cream she uses to make them slighter. She loved to talk about her diet. She didn't like anyone else to talk, and she hated it when Jack and I talked. She loved to make you dust. She loved me.

Kye remembered when hunger was a form of meditation. When you could hear the insides, trilling deliciously under thin skin. When the body was a piece of unimportant rag which nevertheless, obeyed. Which you could treat any way you wanted to and which always responded to any great impulse of your spirit like a disarmed naked woman to the soft of your thumb. When weakness was a strong sensation similar to drinking champagne on an empty stomach. When you wanted to prolong this sensation like you would want to prolong the effects of a drug. When in walking in weakness there was no danger of keeling over, of falling, of losing control. When the sixtieth cigarette and the third bottle did not signify an imminence of death. When, alone, FEAR was cosy.

She looked at you with the eyes of a cow tinged with the

sharpness of a rat's. She brought you salads when you needed meat. Even dry English wooden meat. She was an expert at tarot.

And the hunger he felt was not the way it should be, placed. It was everywhere, it governed his every gesture, every look. Even the lips, hurrying every sentence forward as if it was the last. Before the collapse. Before the final withering. No gongs, no explosion, just a slight crackle of the last withering away of life.

Sleep would help. If sleep was a going out of something into something else. But when Kye slept, his belly remained open for any old boot to march in. To keep his spine pinned to the mattress for a twelve-hour nightmare. It was better trying to stand behind the counter trying to combat the spinning. He would have liked to talk to a lover about her new necklace. He could not talk to Jack about her new perfume for the stench of it. Kye was a polite young man who would not talk about the stench of their new perfume to anybody. But about beads made of exotic wood on a nylon string. About a ring made of miniature railway tracks. He would like to talk about that to a lover. Or even to Jack if Jack was wearing beads on a nylon string or railway tracks on her fingers. But Jack was not the type and she hadn't washed her hair for a week and you couldn't talk to a girl about her unwashed hair even if she was a feminist. He talked to Jack about her new boots and where she got them and that she should buy shoe polish. Haila told Kye that he should dust psychology.

A couple of pints for lunch at the King's Head with a couple of drunks at the bar and a couple of drunks at a table and a couple of eaters. Robin was passing.

Hi, man, we haven't had a dialogue for years.

Hi, Kye said.

Do you like Sartre, Robin said.

No, Kye said.

I think Sartre is great, Robin said. You don't like Sartre, Robin said.

No, Kye said.

I think Sartre's really profound, Robin said. I think Sartre reaches, Robin said. I am skinned, Robin said.

So am I, Kye said.

Can you buy me a pint, Robin said.

Yes, Kye said.

I think Sartre reaches, Robin said. I think Sartre is great, Robin said. You don't like Sartre, Robin said.

No, Kye said.

Thanks, Robin said.

That's alright, Kye said.

I think Sartre reaches, Robin said. You don't think Sartre reaches, Robin said.

Yes, Kye said.

What, Robin said.

Nothing, Kye said.

How are you doing, Robin said.

Fine, Kye said.

I must read this Sartre guy again, Robin said.

Why, Kye said.

To know if he reaches, Robin said.

To stand with a flask of whisky in the shadow of a train waving to mother leaving. Tears in the eyes for the leaving mother. Mother, I cry as the train pulls off, mother I cry. I don't have money for a beer at the Train Bleu, mother I cry, if only I had money for a beer at the Train Bleu, mother I cry as the train pulls off.

Kye remembered when panic was a safe sensation. Like an elastic band cutting into your wrist.

In the shop there was a telephone. Kye phoned Asde to arrange a meeting to talk about German angst which Asde hates. It was nice to talk to Asde about things she hated. She looked cute. And she always had a good bottle of cognac, or a good bottle of scotch, and she drank well. She knew artists.

When you have a full nose blow it.

Down below where the waters are still natural.

Drink your fill.

With natural ease he drifted into the land of one day.

Today his grandmother rotted just like on any other day unless she was a saint which she probably was. In that case when motherland is free thoughts will be directed to excavation. Will they have clothed her in white, virgin that she was? Or will they have added another lie to their preciosity? Clothed her in black like some widow? Like some sorrowing chunk of corruption? Heedless of natural waters and their green effects? Drinking her fill?

There were only two shelves of philosophy to be dusted so he combined it with health.

Somehow mother nature's got it all wrong. Thrust a thermometer in your armpit. You can't Philip Morris jaunes in England. About the other colours I am not so sure. When you have a full nose blow it.

The evening outside was L O V E L Y . Spanish girls fingering themselves on sidewalks. Bittersweet young men of money. Throwing sidelong glances at the sidewalks. Mini-skirted barmaids of uncertain origin. Perfumed belly-buttons bare to the near-frost. Myself, waiting for John, throwing sidelong glances at the sidewalks. In the hotness of Spanish summer I break my nails on London marble. De l'eau gazeuse, s'il vous plait, and thank God you didn't understand and brought me beer. On the unironed shirt of the barmaid an after-work stain from the night before. I smack my lips to let her know my appreciation. She grins at me like Audrey Hepburn and at once I want to be in Rome on vacation. Her ankles dance elusively and I want to lie on the floor with tongue hanging out trying to lick them. John comes. We look at each other mutely he pointing to the bar I nodding. He lies on the floor with his tongue hanging out. I have to calm down Chris the manager. The barmaid, afraid, hides behind a bittersweet young man of money who, afraid, laughs stupidly. John grins like Robert Mitchum and hides his glass in his paw. The merriment is universal. The barmaid

Petra, hips swinging, comes to sit on Johnny's knee. The young man of money is looking around, trying to collect the credit. Hell, I say, Johnny. Johnny beams and, expertly, flicks the contents of his glass over his shoulder in the hero's face. The hero, afraid, appeals to Chris the manager. Chris the manager, serious, explains, that accidents do sometimes happen. Kye, John says, you can't sleep in your dump, Kye. Not tonight you can't sleep in your dump, Kye.

Paintings and sculptures present a slightly nightmarish obstacle course in the semi-darkness of John's house. Slightly heavenly, too, this amalgamation of created objects pro sua generis. A black cat crosses my path which I take to be a sign of luck like one does when stepping in shit, or walking through a mirror. Everything will be fine, this evening anyway, downstairs in the kitchen with me drinking wine and John unsweetened diabetic tea.

Did you know, John, that my grandmother was a diabetic? She was run over by a truck.

As we wait for the water to boil, as I uncork the bottle, I want John to be my father, a father who would pamper me, and I feel like weeping. John, you are like an Old Testament prophet before the coming forth, still nursed on the milk of fat cows on evergreen prairies, before the exploding of anger. Your cheeks are still red and round, and your eyes light up only with gentleness. But the time is near when your giant's hands will strike down the citadels of men. For now they are only good for warming up kittens. But the time is near when your eyes will discharge lightning that no one will be able to conduct, when the thunder of your voice, now only good for rocking babies to sleep, will reverse the poles. Then I will take shelter under your wings and watch the long awaited destruction of the Earth.

Mosquitoes will bite in the long hot summers of the future. Then I will feel whole in my loneliness without the trembling. Then I will feel bitten, accepted, sucked. Millions of lovers will feed on me and I, naked, arms outstretched, will receive them. Glory, they will buzz, glory to the Sole and Only. And I will smile and I will bless them. I will have forgotten the meaning of streets and of windows giving out on to the streets. I will be a pirate with nothing to plunder. I will be a thief with no one to steal from. And I will be happy in my power. Then I will proclaim the Kingdom of John.

Bells rang in the evening drizzle. In the Saturday evening drizzle the first Mass of the Holy Obligation. For those with cars to clean, for the sick in the near future, for entrepreneurs, for the creative forces in society, for policemen. Virgin of the Chains, pray for us as we clutch bead necklaces that we are too ashamed to wear. Give us strength, O Mother of God, to ask your Very Strict Son for forgiveness. The son who said: Be naked.

Visiting mother. In front of the box lying the mother, sprawling in her dirty sheets in her dirty nightshirt munching a bun topped with cold baked beans. Hi mother, hi hi hi hi mother, he wanted to shout and throw himself round her neck and kiss her neck. But the stench of sweat-soaked nylon cut off the vocal tubes and the blob of old tomato on her collar froze him on the doorstep. How is J.R., mother, intellectually analyzed?

There is no food here, son, you should have warned me you were coming. I don't feel like talking. I am tired.

He stood there for a while, watching J.R. munch a bun, one baked bean landing on his crisp white shirt.

Bye, mother.

Bye, son. Next time, phone.

There was a time when I proclaimed things, thought Kye, and a shiver of courage ran up and down his spine. There was a time I wore necklaces for everyone to see, and talked about the Book and the Writer. It used to give me good appetite.

Outside, puddles have begun to collect. The drizzle turned into rain. A few leaves still dangled on the branches of trees, and perennial English roses in perennial English front gardens basked perversely in the cold. There were times when I sang Salve Regina walking in the rain, and licked droplets off the roses, and smiled at the cycle of death.

Robin was sitting at the bar, staring defiantly at the crowd. Hi, man.

Hi.

I've re-read Sartre, man.

Oh yeah.

You were right, man. About Sartre.

Was I?

Yeah. He doesn't reach, man, Sartre, man. Yeah.

He doesn't?

No man, I mean when you read him again he's sort of unreachable man know what I mean? That's what I think.

Can you buy me a pint, Robin?

You never listen man, really. I'm trying to tell you something and you never listen man. Know what I mean. Something that's hit me man about Sartre. I mean the guy is sort of unreachable man he doesn't reach.

He don't reach.

No he don't.

Can you buy me a pint, Robin?

Have you read Bukowski? Kye? Man?

Yeah.

What d'you think?

Can you buy me a pint, Robin?

A pint for my friend here, Jane baby.

Thanks.

I'm broke, you know, man. I mean I'm broke.

Yeah.

What d'you think?

About what?

About Bukowski dammit. Charles Bukowski, man.

Cheers.

Yeah cheers. What do you think?

The beer here is getting worse.

I think he's sort of cool, you know, but a bit anti-women.

Who told you that?

Well. Colette, you know.

Has she read him?

Not really man you know. But she sort of feels it.

It's rubbish.

That's what she said. That it was anti-women rubbish you know, Bukowski, and that I shouldn't read it.

Bukowski isn't rubbish. What she feels is rubbish.

Really? That's what I tried to tell her you know? Man? I mean. Really. He's sort of great isn't he really?

Yeah.

I mean he's GREAT isn't he?

Yeah.

That's just what I told her man. But you know them.

Whom?

Women.

No.

Your turn. You're a great friend, pal, you know that? And Robin put his hand on Kye's receding shoulder.

I have mused about parks. But can you go to a park, on a cold night, in the rain, without a bottle, with fear? In the hope of finding a wounded swallow? Of healing? Better to go home and sweep the floor. Borrow a broom from the other John and sweep it. The crumbs away. Pour the other John's aftershave on the rotting wood to neutralize the stench of piss. Start anew. Without melancholy and the mending of broken wings. New birth in clean surroundings, a home-birth. Take the whisky bottle and wipe it clean of sticky finger marks and put it on a shelf. To neutralize the attraction of squalor. Dust the desk. Look around for something else to do. Critically appraise the result smacking your lips, tongue in cheek. Ah yes, change the sheets, smooth over the bed cover. Straighten up. Look around the walls wishing you had painted them better. Look at the bed. Lick your lips.

Kye walked in the rain, wishing he had a house with a broom of his own. With a shelf to put the whisky bottle on. With a special shelf for the whisky bottle where books would not interfere. He would sit in a chair and look at the bottle and admire it and admire himself not drinking from it. He would soak his feet in hot water looking at the bottle and admiring it. He would have his trousers turned up just above the ankle and wiggle his toes and look at the toes and admire them. Then, drying his feet, not rubbing them, pressing the towel gently to. Putting on a clean pair of socks, sniffing them first to make sure. Roll down the trousers, put on a pre-polished pair of shoes, empty the sink. Back in the room reach for the bottle with deliberation, calmly, without haste. Just one medium glass of the scotch and one cigarette before going out. Before hitting it big.

With the couple of pints in his brain Kye had recovered his equilibrium. He could walk without the fear of leaving a

leg behind, without the otherwise permanent sensation of the imminence of the spilling out of his insides. He wanted to stick out his tongue and taste the rain out of a sort of mechanical memory of a once upon a time joy. He thought better of it, suddenly ecologically conscious. I remember the gas man with his long pole switching on the gas lamps in the eerie dusks of winter. I would open my mouth and swallow. And I wanted to be a gas man. Down below the devils raged and produced — light.

Down here Kye stretched out his hand hoping for a touch of a hand he knew. Of a hand he kissed of a hand he loved of a hand he held close to his belly and close to under his belly. A lamppost dripping with dark liquid smog responded to the invitation.

The bus stop was a large gaping wound waiting for a bandage. Kye's charity not being up to it, he changed course. There was a time when it did not matter which course one took. When every path led to the Rome of unashamed self-discovery. Or an unashamed discovery of another, or of something, or of an emotion, or of emotion. But now every step he took was one of hesitation, of scrutinizing the pavement for excrement.

And he contemplated the underground exit and he thought of a home and he thought of a hole in the ground and he thought of a rabbit. And he turned on his heels and he turned up his collar.

Rain-sodden he re-reached the place of mother. Shivering

he thought of an old tomato and saliva drivelling down her chin. And J.R. indignantly playing to it all. But mother wasn't in. Half a bottle of rum was in, polished, sitting on a shelf. On the unmade bed a naked bean stuck in a position of authority. On the carpet an army of assorted crumbs, a hairpin, a piece of cotton wool. On the table political literature. Kye wished, for a moment, when not looking at the half bottle of rum, that he had mastered his fear of holes and gone to the other place to borrow the other John's broom. Then, remembering essentials he took the bottle and climbed the stairs to his now his brother's room, switched on the light, put on the electric heater, sat down on the mattress with the large cushion not behind his back, stretched his legs, sighed, looked at the low ceiling, looked at the Kertesz poster on the wall opposite, smiled, looked at the spot on the floor where his desk had stood. Memories, like butterflies without the worm in the middle. We made love here, when I had pushed the desk against the wall to make space for another mattress which we didn't need. Mother was out, then, too. And she came, dressed in a dark blue travelling outfit, tired, frightened, insecure, happy. Off the coach she came like that, and she waited for me on a bench because the coach was early. And she was frightened that I wouldn't come and then she knew I would. And she sat there with the luggage between her knees. And she had combed her hair in the toilet and it was smooth and long and shiny. And she sat there with her eyes wide open looking at the crowd looking for me. She sat there like that I remember her and I remember when our eyes met. And when our joys surged and we were shy and hungry for each other. She didn't want to take me by the hand, even, and then she did and we walked hand in hand. And she admired the London cab and laughed at the rude driver and saw colour everywhere. She put her head on my shoulder then and laughed and said she was tired and that her dress was crumpled. I kissed her hand then and I stroked her cheek and her head lay softly between my shoulder and my chin. And I said I had a surprise for her at home. And she said that she was too tired to take in all the colour. And I said we had plenty of time and that we had all our lives. She fell asleep then and I cried and the driver muttered something about frogs. And then once at home I nearly had to carry her upstairs together with the baggage. And the flat was spotless because I had made it so. And in my mother's room there was the surprise there were strawberries and champagne. And she said she was no longer tired but I knew she was but I said of course not how could you be let's drink. Just like in Paris when we woke up and now we can pretend that we have never got out of bed that we have always and I kissed her and pressed her to me and her small breasts were hard and soft against my chest.

Kye, oh Kye, and Kye watched Kertesz's whore through a mist.

Then of course after the first bottle she had to sleep. I couldn't sleep at all so I sat there and I watched her and then

I opened another bottle and watched her some more. She was beautiful when she slept of course and as I watched her I cried some more and I knew that all our lives was but I hoped. I hoped and I dreamt watching her crying like that. I sat on a chair crying like that, bent over to be able to smell her. She smelled wonderful of course whether she slept or whether she waked. I touched her temple with the tips of my fingers and in English I thought of cathedrals and incense and genuflections. And I knelt beside the bed and lifted and spread out my arms and prayed to St. Bernadette not decaying in Nevers. Then I knew our lives together couldn't wouldn't but I hoped. And then I stood up and cursed all the saints and shouted defiance to God and made a bet with Satan. And then I laughed at my bet but I had made it. Satan of course does exist but I laughed at Satan and his existence. And I made it plain to the skies that I hoped in spite of them and because of a cave by the sea. I love you, I whispered in her ear and I lay down beside her and I buried my face in her hair. And falling asleep I smelled her hair and I smelled the skin of her neck.

Kye turned his head from side to side, missing the large gone cushion.

Then tired too I went upstairs not to disturb her sweet smelling sleeping. The same upstairs I am sitting in now, drinking rum. But I wish I was home. But that place isn't a home. Over there was home, once. Where after the girls phoned other friends different friends phoned about different things and different adventures. And there was home in the fighting and in the cutting off of phones. Then I went to sleep.

Asde was particularly hot that night, with a particularly good bottle on the polished shelf. She was full of frivolity, and shyness, and embarrassment, and arrogance. She was her perfect cock-tease self. Fingers playing now with the earlobe, now with the lower lip. Eyes wide open to a clever point you make. Red-coloured laughter. Crossing her legs she touches your calf with the tip of her toe. Red-coloured smile and the lowering and narrowing of the eyes. When something remembered a hand on your knee and then a sharp reclination and the bow of the neck. And then the conversation turned sour, and then the conversation turned sweet. And the sourness meant nothing, and the sweetness meant nothing. And it was a relief. Five hours of drinking to get drunk and of a conversation which was totally forgettable, a plunging into a warm senseless plasma. And Asde ate something and I didn't eat anything. And I loved the shrinking of the stomach and the lightness of the brain and I didn't think of the bones piercing the skin on my shoulders. About politics we talked about art we talked in a delirium of clichés. And we laughed and we shouted and we didn't mean the laughing and we didn't mean the shouting. And we hugged each other and we kissed each other and we didn't mean the hugging and we didn't mean the kissing. And we talked about our hair and we talked about our clothes and about the hair and the clothes of others. And we bitched about our friends as later we would bitch about each other with our friends. And it was a glorious night and in the morning I took a taxi home. And before I took a taxi home we joked about being lovers.

And in the morning when I awoke I thought I would not be able to get up. But I got up and in my trembling I went to work. Sweating and shaking I went to work and I still had time to have a drink at the Head. And I didn't see the drunks just as I hadn't seen the dirt on the floor in the morning. And Haila was cool and said I should eat more and Jack was cool. Jack you are cool and you eat enough and you smell and maybe in another life you believe in other lives I liked that smell I ran around the whole world trying to smell that smell Jackie. You have beautiful eyes Jack and you are tough and you are lost and you are thirty but you look twenty-three. And I dust poetry and I flick through E.E. Cummings and Haila tells me not to read at work but I say that I am flicking through the pages to make them clean. And when I get up from the dusting my head spins and I hold on to the shelving and a customer smiles at me and I smile back in my trembling and nobody notices the wet marks of my fingers on the waxed false wood. And at lunch I go to the Head and eat a hamburger in my spinning and drink a pint to stop the spinning. And artists talk to me about art.

Where, in the hell, am I?

And I pose the question to myself as I drink a second pint at a gallop but I know I am suspended between a somewhere which is no longer either a some or a where and another where which consists entirely of anti-sentiments. But I drink my beer not daring to probe too deeply preferring to stay with the first question of Where, in the hell, am I? Does it matter WHERE in hell one is? Confusion arises with the stupid hope that there is a place outside of hell, that there is a SOMEWHERE. But the hamburger was good and the beer was good although I would have to piss a lot and leave the shop a lot to go piss in the leaking toilet in the back but which is good because that way I will smoke cigarettes. And I said goodbye to the artists who said that we should talk a lot more about art and that in that there is hope. And so I went back to the shop covering my face from the stinging rain.

Rose-coloured nymphets, I would like to burrow through your tiny hearts with nostrils full of blood. Thus redeemed I Kye would recover his greatness. Session after session I would tear open your breasts, leaving my eyes open to better savour the beauty. And you will feel grateful to me, and you will feel justified. Ah, I am not saying this in anger. And I offer you, kissing your bare flesh through the hole in your jeans, Wuthering Heights, freely. Hide them in your trousers and you will keep them warm.

There is a place where the statutes of liberty are being evoked. Against non-liberty. Then there is this place. But I flick through Naughty Dots. I want to sit in an armchair with a Havana cigar and join the dots to create lines. Then, legs spread trousers down just enough to show the crotch I would make my tool work. I need to pee on account of the two beers at the Head and I go to the back and I pee and I make my tool work and I have a cigarette. Next time it will be Samantha Fox wrapped in celophane who will ease the bulging. But now I smoke my cigarette and I am making coffee for everyone and Haila comes in and is satisfied that I am making coffee for everyone. And Jackie likes hers white as sperm and weak as ejaculation précoce. Oh Jack, Jack, if I had a portrait of yours I would glue it between the blond cascades of Samantha Fox's glorious visage.

When the day is gone. It never used to be gone, the day. It used to go round the clock, once, the day. But now it is divided into light, and dark, into finishing, and recommencing. It is cut up, it is unwhole. Enslaved time has creeped its way into my doing and into my not doing. Enslaved time from dot to dot in the morning, from dot to dot in the night. And pencils are hard to get.

When the day is gone and the key in the hole and the last charmed smiles and the going in separate ways but then — Kye, Haila says, I don't know how to say this but would you — come with me for a drink. And she blushes and throws back her mane of Polish blondness.

But Haila, I have no money.

But it doesn't. It doesn't matter, you know.

With pleasure, Haila.

I am the boss, says Haila, glancing timidly at a pair of millionaire goths sitting opposite us at the table.

Yes.

But I don't want to be the boss, Kye.

I know.

It makes me feel sick being the boss.

Yes.

Really sick.

I know.

Do you resent me for being your boss, Kye?

No.

I am not cut out to be a boss.

No.

I am cut out to be something else.

Yes.

Something more.

No doubt.

But what? I mean who am I? I am ugly, look.

You have beautiful hands.

Do I? Do I blush?

Yes.

My boyfriend said he wished he could fuck my mind.

That's bad.

I mean I have a long neck.

—

I have fat thighs.

—

I have flat feet.
You have beautiful hands.
Do I?
You blush.
I know.
You are pretty when you blush.
Am I blushing now?
Yes.
I told my mother about you.
You did.
My mother is an alcoholic.
—

She would like to meet you.
I would like to be a millionaire goth.
She.
—

Thinks I should get married.
Haila, you are a good boss. You are a good, humane sort of boss.
But I don't want to be a boss, Kye. I want love, every day I search for love every day I read my cards in my search for love which is all I want please order another beer it's on me I know you don't have any money I have it it doesn't matter let's drink it's rare when I can talk to somebody like you and I don't want to be your boss how can I be your boss I mean it's crazy how can I be your boss. Kye.
Haila.

Kye.

It's late.

No it's not we can have a couple more beers and then we can
go somewhere else to drink some more I know I should
watch my figure it's not good for my figure this drinking but
what the hell I've never had such a good time talking to
someone how can I be your boss Kye maybe we can go to my
place afterwards even though I know it's far all the way in
South London I couldn't ask you to go to my place could I?

It's far.

Look here is the beer order another round straight away
there is no hurry to get home but they'll close soon it's not all
that far you know I do it every day sometimes I curse but I
drink hot milk every morning I'd rather not drink coffee it's
bad for your heart at work I drink coffee it's bad for my heart
but you make it so I drink it five cups sometimes a day alcohol is bad for your heart but I drink it because when I drink it
with you I have such a good time and we talk like I've never
talked to anyone in my life look and I am drinking beer I
used to only drink cocktails from time to time my mother is
an alcoholic she is Polish she drinks vodka I didn't want to
become an alcoholic like her but with you it's different she
drinks alone and we are not drinking vodka we are drinking
beer although beer is really bad for your figure but it's good
for your skin I could sit here for hours drinking beer with
you but look they are calling out last orders already I wish we
were on the continent now we are both from the continent

you and I though you know more of the continent than I do you've lived there bars open all night but I think it stays in your blood do you think it stays in your blood the continent I don't know I suppose I am still Polish I have uncles and aunts in Poland I might go visit them would you like to go with or you can't they wouldn't let you in or maybe they would what with what's happening is it really happening Kye sometimes I get so excited about it even though I can't speak the language you know my mother should have taught me but she is an alcoholic and anyway and my father is a sailor always at sea my mother left me to be brought up by strangers until I was nine I guess she couldn't handle it though she says she's always loved me and then she took me back anyway when I was nine I was so happy when she took me back I cried for sure I don't remember but I cried for sure I loved my mother my mother was an alcoholic drinking alone drinking vodka not like the two of us now drinking beer talking look they are shouting at people to get out hell I don't understand it my mother says I should get married I should have been married a long time ago but I guess and she guesses I just had to wait for the right guy she loves Czechs she has a guilt about Czechs about the Second World War and '68 and you speak the language she says it's great you speak the language I think it's great you speak the language I am a Pole you are a Czech she wishes my mother she'd taught me the language but I can still learn it when I go back you never lose your blood or does blood exist I mean a nation's blood the blood of a child and a nation when the child hopelessly bound comes back if he or she comes back to the womb of the Motherland picks up the mothertongue I haven't finished my beer yet waiter thank you I know it's past eleven just let me finish my drink thank you there you are Kye I never used to be so forward so cocky you might say is all this bothering you?

Kye was bothered by Haila's footballs of knees as squatting on the cushions on the floor she showed them to him saying Look Kye how can anybody love me with knees like that. Kye looked at the knees and was disgusted by them and then by his own disgust. Touch them, Haila said to him, feel them they are like footballs. She squatted there in her underpants in her shirt with a can of Hofmeister in her hand rocking back and forth. With her left hand she squashed her left knee Squash it Kye feel it it's like a football. Or like an over-ripe pear she laughed maybe it will burst and pus will come out. Pus will spurt out and cover your face maybe I am sorry I shouldn't be so vulgar. You don't want to touch them anyway who'd want to touch the stupid things but I've been to so many doctors and no one has the answer. Kye sat there denting an empty can popping the dents up and felt pity and felt disgusted by his pity and said Haila maybe one day you will go to Poland and there will be a man waiting for you who will love you. Never, Haila said lying down on the cushions pulling the blanket over her head spilling the beer. And in the dark Kye heard her cry and then he heard her masturbate.

He woke up in the afternoon, not having gone to work. He was bored with his hunger and with his trembling and with his drinking. He was bored with his sleeping and with his wanking. Yet he did not play games. He could not stop it. He was not trying to kill himself, he was sure of that, he did not wish to die. Yet he could not stop it. He simply somehow lost balance. The half of a half bottle of scotch sat amongst dirty socks grinning an invitation taken.

Denise came back from her after-lunch swim, Denise who lived with him in the dog-piss, Denise who laughed, who wore funny hats, who wore tracksuits, who played the bass, who had thick jet black long hair, who was Jewish, who had thick dark eyebrows, who was tiny, who had thick deep sad dark eyes, who did karate, who listened to house, who was always on the verge of losing it but never did because she never stopped running. Denise helped Kye stand.

Come Kye get up stand up clean up let's get out.

Let's go for a pint.

And you'll eat a couple of bangers and mash.

Guinness has a lot of iron in it.

I'm sick of everything Kye. You should quit the shop.

They never talked much, Denise and Kye. They sat in a pub, Kye ate a couple of bangers and mash and drank a pint of iron-giving Guinness. Denise drank a pint of chemical-giving Lamot. You are a friend, Denise.

You are a friend too, you know, Kye.

The swim.

Was nice.

I should go swimming with you.

You should.

One day.

Tomorrow.

I didn't go to work today.

You should quit the shop.

They walked the streets like lovers, with Kye forgetting the loss of balance.

You should take me to one of those clubs, Denise.

I thought you hated them.

You should take me to one.

They flick their forearms up and down to acid.

Why do you go?

They walked fast, and they talked slowly, and they leaned on each other. And the streets were terribly sad, but caressing, like a mother would caress a dying child. Tramps looked away not daring to beg. Respectable people whispered to other respectable people. Camden trendies huddled together.

Let's go pick up some shit.

The asphalt cracked and the street became a slow, black river. White corpses swam in it, corpses that seemed alive, pushed by the undercurrents. I knew them all, and I counted them one by one, to see if anyone was missing. They were all there, my friends. The poet who died of malnutrition in a New York ›hotel‹, the film-maker who drowned himself in cognac after twenty years of silence, the woman gardener

who fell on her scissors as she picked a rose for her lover, the boy who slit his wrists in a passage off a heroes' square, the dancer who broke her spine as she cracked up in mid-air, the one-armed roof-layer whose hook got loose, the young soldier who shot a blank at his sergeant, the prisoner on the sixty-third day of hunger, the young girl in the joys of procreation, the priest when the host shed blood, the male nurse when they opened up his mother, the mother of seven too old to bear an eighth, my brother, and all the saints.

We got some shit from a shit seller, sat shivering on a park bench, smoked some. I don't like shit I don't normally smoke it. Denise likes it Denise smokes it when Denise smokes it I sometimes smoke it. On the park bench we smoked it shivering we didn't feel happy. But we felt together we thought of cadavers. We smoked it she put it in her pocket we were thirsty we went to some pub to drink some beer. We drank it we drank another beer I took some money out of my pocket I paid for it we walked out into the street we thought of cadavers. We went to some pub to drink some whisky not to think of cadavers to think of living beings we drank it. To think of living beings we drank it looking at each other not thinking of each other as living beings. We drank another whisky Denise took some money out of her pocket she paid for it we walked out into the street thinking of cadavers. Walking in this street we were tired we took some bus to some centre. In this centre we didn't walk much we walked a few paces to some central pub trying to find some central laughter. Looking at each other in this pub drinking some port we laughed thinking of cadavers we laughed. All these people are going to flick their forearms to acid later Denise said she emptied her port she wanted another glass to drink. I said I was being careful that too much port she said she liked port at this hour I went to the bar to catch the eye of the pock-marked gentleman to order port. The pock-marked gentleman looked at me didn't like the look of me didn't want to serve me I got cross. Don't look cross the pock-marked gentleman said looking at me not liking me you motherfucker or else. I said give me two glasses of port ugly man. He said if you don't get the fuck out of here you fucking frog fucker I'll fuck the fuck out of you son of a fuck. I said Denise took me by the sleeve dragged me out of the central pub into the central street she didn't want to spend the night at the hospital Denise said. I was very angry in that street I said I should have hit the ugly man she said he would have killed you stupid. We were up in mountain meadows catching yellow butterflies what Denise said I said once we did that Denise said she wished she could remember something like that instead of Canary Islands with her paraplegic sister. I said I have never been to Canary Islands would very much like to have gone would still very much like to if occasion. Troubleshooter. What? That's what I'd like to have been Denise said maybe that's what I am. You shoot me out of trouble that's for sure Denise I said let's cross over the road to avoid the skins. Skins are alright Denise said if you are not alone if it's not two in the morning if you are not in Tottenham skins are alright hi she said to the skins hi they said. You should have been Calamity Jane my God Denise I don't like cowboys Denise said I'd rather have been Mata Hari but I guess I haven't got the build. The pubs were closing it had to be eleven pock-marked men everywhere downing last pints collecting empty pints. Needing to go to the toilet we entered one of the closing pubs to the roar of last orders pushed our way through the throng under the raised beers cheering the royal couple to our relief. Back out in the street Denise was with a rock star friend not looking like a star not looking like a rock hi I said I'm Kye who are you. He looked at me like the pock-marked gentleman in the central pub not liking me he looked at Denise he said who is this I got cross I said don't talk about me behind my back to my friends he said Denise are you coming? Denise said to me he is alright Denise said to him he is alright don't you both be stupid let's go where are we going. He looked at me still not liking me but not so completely not like the pock-marked gentleman in the central pub he said to some fucking stupid charity shit I've got tickets. Charity shit I was afraid more hashish had to be smoked I didn't want to smoke any more hashish Denise said it was a different sort of shit she took a swig from the rock star's coca cola bottle she handed it to me I took a swig shit the damn thing was half scotch. She took the bottle back she took a swig she said to him don't look at him like that he's alright really he's more crazy than you'd think he's crazier than the whole lot of you in fact stop looking at him like that. He was cross with Denise he gave her a look I said don't be cross with Denise who are you anyway? He said fuck the both of you he marched off he came back for the bottle Denise told him to march off. Alone again we were happy we laughed we felt like living beings in this centre which was no longer a centre it was half past eleven. We took a bus Denise knew a gay club Denise said gays are alright even in Tottenham at two o'clock in the morning. The gays were alright they flicked their forearms to acid Denise flicked her forearms to acid I sat at a table with a pint I smiled I was happy I was a living being I smiled at the boys the boys smiled back I wasn't pestered I was with a lady Denise wasn't pestered she smiled at the boys they smiled back. A painted boy sat down next to me smiled at me explained to me that I was in fact gay that I should realize myself I said I was realized I said he stank of perfume I said to leave me alone he got cross he put his hand on my thigh he squeezed it I put my hand on his face he bit it I knocked his drink over into his lap he cried I got up to go he held me by the wrist I pulled him by the hair he looked at me he smiled he cried please don't go please sit down please forgive me I sat down on the edge of my chair he said he was lost I sat there as he cried head down forgetting me fingering wet trousers. Kye! Denise joined me with a couple of other boys Mike! she cried at my crying boy Mike looked up wiped off his tears pursed his lips said Denishe this one here is a hard cookie aren't you dear. Outside the air was pleasant and cool.

Ducks opened their beaks trying to make themselves heard in a park roaring with a north bound artery. Only when standing right by the edge of the pond Kye could hear the quacking. What do they quack about what do they brag about these birds from other continents why don't they stay at home. Who wants them here. They swim in our ponds they eat our worms they waddle in our mud. Quack. Waddle waddle. I should have a shotgun to shoot them to leave them rot who wants to eat their foreign flesh. Who wants them here. We need white ducks with clipped wings, properly stuffed, properly stuffed white geese too on farms. A white girl in a white rabbit fur coat sat down on a bench by the pond uncovering her fish-net-stockinged legs. She must be cold the poor darling Kye thought I wish I had the courage to warm her up. She didn't hear the ducks quack she had ear-phones on her ears a walkman in her lap. Wise. I wish she could prop me up. It is harder and harder to walk.

Friends are harder and harder to get.

There was a time when Kye ate homemade goulash from a big pot with twenty friends in the middle of mountains covered in snow. Reading Lao Tse.

Mornings are harder and harder to take.

There was a time when this wonderful nervousness of anticipation in the guts the evening before the morning before the new day. When surely someone would be loved, or arrested, or beaten. When surely something would happen.

When you wake up in the afternoon after a twelve hour sleep the cigarette doesn't taste good. He used to wake up at five in the morning after a five hour sleep and the cigarette tasted good. It would still be dark it would be freezing the snow would squeak under his feet. His teeth would chatter would twitch the insides of his nostrils would be white tight with frost. His toes would be cold. The tips of his fingers would be cold. He would wear his father's old coat with the torn fur lining with the warm fur collar. He would have long hair white with frost on the forehead with the breathing of his mouth. He would walk fast in the snow keeping his head down tucked in the warm fur collar.

Not having the courage to warm her up not having the courage to ask her to prop him up he walked to the other side of the pond hiding behind the shrub-covered island. Then crawling by the park fence he made his way upstream of the foul breaths of exhaust pipes.

Travelling with a broken nose is easy. Even limping with a leg cut off, compared to this. Take a beggar in a summer meadow.

No, take a black beauty in a summer meadow with her breasts hard with excitement having been raped. Take this wildness.

By Kye.

In the disguise of muscle and sure feet.

Promote the multiplication of cowardice.

Several years later, proud in his groin.

When the trembling and the clutching at fences had stopped.

Proud in his resurrected chest.

Drinking wine with uncontracted stomach.

No longer afraid of madness.

Limbs limp hanging from the chair in the sheer strength.

On the porch of a sheer house.

Content.

With a cigar in his fucking mouth fucking dead.

Pleasant winter afternoons are hard to come by. This was a pleasant winter afternoon. The rain had stopped. The air was wet. And warm. The sun peered through a mist. It could have been romantic. If there was a romance. Chance would bring Kye a romance in nine days. So say the prophets. Would it also be on a pleasant hard to come by winter afternoon?

It was a lousy winter evening. It pissed down with rain. He had lost his umbrella. It was better to stay put. He wished he had a cat. And a blanket. To cover his knees with. And a red-hot stove.

There were once things to get to the bottom of on lousy winter nights. When you could still go back up. The sound of God's piss is sad. My skull will break open. I wish I had a cat to lick the brain out.

Listen to the silence scream. Like my baby. Like my little

baby daughter.

Sweat in my armpits and in my boots as I sit in the rushing train, through nonexistent borders. From sameness to sameness. From hooligans. From businessmen. From happiness in riches. From Coca cola. From misery in front of TV sets. To hooligans. To businessmen. To happiness in riches. To Coca cola. To misery in front of TV sets. And God saw what he had made and it was good. And he pissed on it to make it multiply, and then in his incontinence to drown it. And he saw the drowning of it and he said to Noah, Build a boat.

But listen to my baby daughter scream.

The next day it was a lousy winter morning. Lousy winter mornings are harder and harder to take. Some blackbird had the insolence to sing. Without even the white snow for pleasing contrast. When in the winter it snows in the morning then the morning is not lousy but beautiful and soft and gentle and mysterious and fabulous. Especially when you are a kid like Kye once was in the unnameable backthere. But it was raining like it did in the night and in the evening and in the afternoon and in the morning the day before. And no more thoughts. Walking with the useless umbrella in the lashing wind Kye walked to the bus stop to take the bus to work to dust astrology. Stars that once connected some one to another one now gathered together a bundle of scared cooks. Or the eaters of the meals of these cooks praying that in their pre-ordained luck they will not be poisoned. Since perhaps you can buy the stars just like you can buy the books about the stars and get them ON YOUR SIDE. Or they can get them on their side. Kye with no more thoughts sat on the upper deck of the steamy smoky double decker bus staring at the roofs of the rows of squatting houses not being able to smoke like he used to be able to smoke first thing in the morning with pleasure sucking the smoke deep in the healthy lungs but trying to anyway. And above the water was a head. What? So soon? The muscular shoulders from time to time emerging having propelled flung back the no doubt muscular arms to propel fling forward the muscular body with the help of the muscular thighs. What? Rushing down the steps jumping out just in time nearly collapsing on the very pavement with the very effort.

Stars, Haila said opening a book in the middle, you cannot do without the stars. There is. Everything. Look. But you are not allowed to read while you dust. This year for me is full of misery, and so was last year, and so was the year before last, and so were all the years before the year before last. Look. But you are not allowed to read while you work. Even my knees are in the stars, and she turned a few pages over. Look. Where is my rep?

The muscular swimmer, having swum across the English Channel, covered in white foam, breathing heavily like I do at the top of a flight of stairs. He had trained himself by keeping his head in a sink full of salted water. For where he came from there were only sweet-tasting lakes and down-ward-rushing sweeter-smelling rapids of narrow medium height mountain rivers. He had trained himself by swimming up the rapids, like the salmon he had seen in risky shiny foreign journals. Between the breasts of femmes sublimes.

The blood or whatever it is buzzing in the skull. The sweat or whatever it is cascading down protruding ribs, rapid-like. The dust from the books filling the nostrils. I am a Paris-Dakar hero.

John, your strong forearms under my shoulder half carrying me through the streets. The exhausted driver of a vehicle half buried in a desert dune. Not the swimmer, now. No salty water anywhere to lie in or to fight. Just breathing in the dust now, and no white embroidered ladies handkerchief to stain with the black soot. And I am not leaning on you like I would on a stick but I let myself be carried by you like a half broken doll. Did you use to play with your sister's dolls John or do you have a sister? If I had a sister John I would have played with her dolls for sure. But the buzzing in the skull of a doll John? Is it the echo of gun shots? May I ask, may I ask where?, to which watering hole? but it doesn't matter just lift me up a little more so my sore feet are off the beaten ground.

Take a dog collar. You can take a dog collar and you can put it round a naked woman's neck and you can take a picture of her being led by a middle aged gentleman in a business suit. You make money and you are sure to get a hard-on. But you can't lift her up by the dog collar unless you want to finish her off having done it. To lift her up without finishing her off to lift her up like she was stuffed with feathers like they do it in the movies you need a strong arm like yours. Eh John? To lift her up?

Oh Kye.

No really John in this watering hole there are plenty of women we can strip and then you can lift them up like they were stuffed full of feathers and I can take a picture of it and then you can take a picture of me leading them on a leash attached to the dog collar and then if we want to finish them off you can just lift them up by the dog collar and I can take a picture of that too.

Oh Kye.

No really John.

Excuse me, please, thank you.

That's alright.

Lucy had foul breath.

Trembling on a winter break with Lucy in Dorset in the warm wind. Staring dizzily at the high waves. Listening to the crashing. Wondering how the stones can. Day in and day out. Getting a foot licked on the slanting Cobb. Balance restored in the danger. Wet in the warm wind, salt drops and sweet drops mixed. From the clouds in the sky and from the mirrored image in the greyness. Mixed also in the palms of his hands the drops from within and the drops from without. Unoccupied pebble beaches walking heavily in the pebbles. Muscles straining with the pleasure of it. Boarded up huts thoughts of squatting in one of the huts. Muscles straining with the unboarding of it. With the pleasure of it. Thoughts of hermits.

Fishermen's boats in the harbour. Trembling under the impact of wavelets. Of what had once been mighty waves. Out beyond the stones. Before the crashing of them. And the day in of it all, and the day out of it. And the standing of Kye in the midst of it.

The unmooring of one of the boats, with well wide shoulder blades with a good layer of sinewy meat atop the structure. Then out into the wild seas beyond the stones and not trembling any more but swaying. And singing into the swaying. And hoping in the midst of it.

But instead of a boarded up hut an old pink cottage. One of a row. Thatched roof and TV to boot. But the prettiest. And outside the window concrete and beyond the concrete rocks and beyond the rocks the sea. Only no Kye outside on the sea on an unmoored boat swaying. Inside on the contrary in the warmth slicing up Somerset brie trying not to get too close to Lucy's mouth did you have a nice walk yes. By the warmth of the electric fire the question wish there was a fireplace here. After all the thatched roof. After all the thick walls the renting out of the thick walls in the winter to solitude seeking couples. The stench of old perfume too hovers here in spite of the airing they must have given the house after the end of the summer. Together with the dusting of the pictures of she-dogs standing on hind legs full frontal. With the pictures of Mary Magdalens and Marys the Mothers of Jesuses of Lourdes. With the nipple-squeezing Bronzino. No matter, it is cosy. Though I would like to see a crucifix on the kitchen wall for emphasis. Or at least the beheading of St. Cath. Or the martyrdom of St. Seb. Or some such like. For the proper contrast. For the pious wriggling of the arse in an armchair.

Standing on the concrete just outside the door in the wind, dry, I observe the clouds swallowing stars. But the stars always come out through the rear end, untarnished. After-dinner alchemy.

After dinner Lucy wanted to stay inside, in the cosiness. I wanted to see if I couldn't spot the Swimmer. But hey, this is surely far too wide even for him to cross. Or am I underestimating him? And anyway, it is dark. Or has he got a miner's helmet on? Leading sailors astray, capsizing warships? Vain thoughts. Yet if I were to see the light, would I meet it? I cross the concrete cliff to stand by the railing to hold on to it to look at the white foam down below to feel the occasional drop splatter on my face. Would I meet it? Would I rush towards it? Vain thoughts. Yet. Slippery and greased-up arms of the Swimmer. Nothing much to hold on to, after having plunged into the cold dark waves, after having braved the tide, after having met the light.

Behind the closed doors back in the warmth the roaring of the waves intensified by the echo of the walls. By the screening. Stalling the bedward drive of Lucy's amorous gaze. Holding on to the bottle. Pleading the beauty of fires be it electric, and of armchairs of ground floors of ancient cottages be it not so ancient. Pouring her a glass, forcing her to drink it slowly in the bliss of detached privacy. Extolling the preciousness of passions calmed down, of peace, of immobility. Of the need of the nervous city dweller to — do nothing. From time to time. In the country. At least on the first night in the country to do it. The nothing. To just sit movelessly gazing at the night outside, listening to the roar of the sea outside, doing nothing. Just sitting and drinking and gazing and hearing. Just letting the jerky muscles recover some litheness. On the first night. That followed by a day of intense walking, of scaling cliffs, of breathing in the ocean. To let some iron seep in. Then on the second night the rewards reaped in the fulfillment of desire. And Lucy, mouth hanging open, corners of mouth stabbing the chin, eyes contemptuous, climbed the stairs to the bedroom. And Kye marvelled at the deftness of his arguments, and at the truth of them, and the tension at last left his body. And on the morrow he did walk intensely, and he did scale cliffs, and he did breathe in the ocean. And through the trembling and through the sweating the iron did seep in and he stood there, in the wind, solid, lord.

The grass bent, sharp blades piercing the skin just above the ankles, just where the boot stopped, through the thin sock or just above it. The blood, not stooping down to taste it, trickled over the thin sock, and into the boot just below it. Cigarette impossible to light to add to the drama due to the wind even when cowered squatting with his back to the wind. Lungs free from inside influence therefore and then the lifting of feet to walk up a mound of earth and then down it back down to the beach through the shrubs a different way this time steep slopes sliding down on the clay on the wetting arse tufts of grass stuck to the arse green on blue. Laughs from the belly face contorted as branches slashing about. Then finally the final drop no more than two meters O.K. down on the feet then on to the head then on to the back first clay then sand then smallstones. Then looking at the sea then not the courage to go in. Then orientation. Good at. Forbidden boy scouts back there. In the orient. Orifice open now tasting the salt haze. Eyelashes stuck to eyebrows taking in the greyness. Visibility not more than a sprinter's effort. To strain in the sight the wonderful feeling therefore of not being able to catch it. The something. Him. Miners' helmets are made for blackness. Then left he turned eastward he turned pebbles screeching like teeth in gums surrendered. Would pick up a starfish on the way if there were any this far north. Sharks' fins too he would spot on the ninety-ninth meter mark. Meanwhile dark descends climb over two boulders God's droppings to see the lights of the port in the distance. Then relax the gait. Then drop the shoulders then let the arms dangle in the wind. Then let the calves do their own propelling. Then rejoice at the well-oiled knee-joints. Still, he thought hitting the Cobb with a well-aimed stone, forgetting her breath, I would like to have brought her back a starfish.

Remembering her breath, rejoicing at the nonraining, he climbed the steps on to the Cobb, rejoiced at the slanting towards the water of it, walked to where it began to bend, sat down with his back to the roaring, faced the line of pale blue and pink interchangeable now under the light of orange streetlamps, and watched with a smile the one yellow light burning in only one of the line. Somebody else was sitting in the cosy room, burning that light. There was a real fireplace there, too, you could see the shadows dancing on the walls. She sat there, toes playing with the flames, drawing the heat towards her, the tongues of the fire kissing her bare neck, never harming her, just softly, softly, causing her to purr. Her almond-coloured hair, her almond-coloured eyes, her olive skin, alive in the glow. Alive with a thousand lives, each one giving thanks to its Maker. But the Maker of those Lives was the Woman. And I, the Invisible Man, kneeling, just watching, watching the slender fingers of her right hand touch her right temple, to slide over her cheekbone, to rest, for a moment, on her lips. Yet there was a time when I. Touched.

The wet arse from the wet clay was getting wetter. No stars so desired to be seen to prolong the vigil. The getting up on the feet difficult stiff with the cold the circulation cut off just above the knee the legs having dangled in the air. Thoughts in the confines of the skull again, dragging a moon from the firmament. Bloody rain again.

Treble the effort as, leaping over the railing you stand in front of the door, joyful in the anticipation of goodness. Knock twice. The door opens and you, in the anticipation, hide your nose in the sleeve of your coat.

The door opened and closed, Kye ducking to untie his muddied boots. Straightening up stretching his toes Kye strode firmly to the other side of the room to put his muddied coat on the hanger. Kye stopped to pause to admire the spiral staircase under which the hanger was to be found. Kye said it was a beautiful spiral staircase and that it reminded him of the spirals of the paths leading up the ravaged cliffs to give in to smooth grass at the top. Kye described how firmly he stood up on top in the wind, heedless of the stinging blades. Kye described how pure his lungs felt purer than at any time since the long mountain ridge walks back in the but he had to stop himself he didn't want to reminisce. Standing close to the electric fire flaking off dry mud from his trousers on to yesterday's newspaper he said he didn't want to reminisce. With his back to Lucy arms downstretched palms at right angles to forearms he didn't want to. Only the warmth of the fire when he closed his eyes reminded him of. But anyway Lucy how was your day. Lucy had cooked dinner had fried courgettes had burnt them had had to throw it all away. Too late now to go shopping again had cried about it. Hates that sort of thing when that sort of thing happens. Had bought cheese and bread however and wine. Feels now again like crying about it all again. Don't cry Lucy it's not worth it. Kye doesn't like fried courgettes anyway, nor baked nor boiled courgettes. But she does. With two firm strides Kye was in the kitchen cutting some crumbly bread sticking frozen lumps of butter on the uneven surface placing the slices evenly on an oval shaped plate placing the cheese separately on a smaller round shaped plate. Carried it all to the small coffee table not to the large dining table. Went back to the kitchen came back with two glasses and a bottle. Opened the bottle poured the wine into the glasses. Why, Lucy asked, are we eating here rather than at the dining table properly so provided. To be more intimate, Kye replied, glad at the distance separating one reclining head in an armchair from another. And anyway how was your day, Lucy, Kye asked, sipping some wine lighting a cigarette leaving the butter to melt a little. Then, looking at the ceiling blowing smoke at the ceiling he said, This is my first one. And it tastes better than at any time since. What? what? what?, Lucy wondered.

With her mouth full Lucy wondered, spitting out liquidized bread and cheese and butter as she did the wondering. And the cheese flew the furthest landing on Kye's now mudless knee. Well never mind, Kye said, quickly finishing his glass, pushing the splattered plates of food away from him. Then, pulling a crumpled bit of toilet paper from out of his pocket, he wiped the oral dropping from his now mud-free knee. But you must finish your sentences when you talk to me. But you must. And you should eat something.

Bells rang in his ears as he looked past Lucy's shoulder at the dark wet shining window-pane. Can you hear them, Lucy? Profound musical shudders summoning the people to God, and he would run down the boulevard to obey the summons. Or is it all in my head? Then in the church he would stand listening as the sound floated back to Heaven. To give way to silence. Then to words and music that could not be heard from Outside. Then to peace and strength and tears of joy. Can you hear it, Lucy? Then he watched the drops making their way erratically down the outer side of the glass. Or is it all in my head?

Or is it all? Tangible spiders made of goats' liver? Elephant horse-dogs? Hornets? Dracula-like cyclists disturbing the freedom of speech? Sealed letterboxes? Skin hunters?

Growing pains in the nervousness of summer. As boys turned into men down in the groin. Companions in sticky flies we found it difficult to run. Except when the wasps got hungry for an aimless sting. This is what I remember. The desire. For a painted mouth for the flutter of blackened lashes for the simmer of pale blue eyelids. Of a girl recently scorned. For her hips now discovered. For the tightness of her jeans. For the looseness of her blouse and for her breasts and for the drop of perfume in between. For her slut's voice.

Love had changed.

Reminiscing thus, Kye performed the act to the roar of angry English waves. With his nose buried in the pillow. And Lucy, content, kept the semen in till morn.

And as she drove Kye thought of love changing. From for the child to for the woman. From the plump cheeks and from the smell of a babe. From the formless movements. From the wileless smile. From unambiguous laughter. From touching without rousing. From star-gazing to other-gazing.

And as she drove she spoke. And Kye didn't listen. And London loomed.

A McDonald's dinner, heavy in the stomach, lighter in the wind. Through the open window lighter in the wind it went, careful not to spoil the car-mother covers of the seats. Yes, and then the trembling recommenced. Yet I had walked in the fresh air, I had eaten well, climbed cliffs, no less, braved the tides. Yet I Kye had been a strong man by the sea, and passing fathers had told their sons look son pointing at me, here is a strong young man, be like him. Now back to the same, gasping for air, feeling the skin of the stomach touch the spine. Hands sweating again, wetting false leather, persistent itching under life-lines. Toes of feet curling, wriggling, cringing from the rising tides of shoe-confined mud-baths. Pearly droplets on forehead and nose, too numerous to be elegant. Sounds shots in the skull, bouncing from side to side, from back to front. Heart, furiously drumming at the rib cage, lung-shudders for background, eyes, watering, unable to distinguish any longer, objects, meaningless, Lucy I must be dying.

Soup.

What?

I'll cook some soup.

Yes.

When we get home.

O yes.

Soup, comforting, a bouillon, chicken stock with rice, just like mother used to, or noodles, good for you, get it down you, after a day's running about, just like a child does run about, to build up an appetite, not to quench it, not to satisfy it, or even later, when grown up, after a day's of metaphorical running about, of doing things, of being alive, of coming home, not to lie down, not to eat the soup to lie down after coming home, but to build up an appetite, not for more food, but for more doing things, for more running about, for more being alive. Coming home.

The car stopped in the lively quartier of Stoke Newington backstreets. A mongrel defecated on the pavement. A lady owner peeped from behind a curtain. A lass cursed a lad. A lad struck a lass. A lad's arse stuck out from an engine. All is well.

The soup was good. After the soup came Honey, and Lucy's face drew near. Now pay for it. But Kye couldn't. I can't Lucy.

Why not?

Don't know. Just can't.

Am I not attractive? To you?

No you are. You are.

Well then?

Don't love you Lucy. Am sorry. Meant to tell you earlier. Am sorry. Felt very sick. As you've seen. Thanks for the soup. It was lovely. Almost like my mother used to. Am sorry. Lucy. Baaastaard.

Then at him she came, for his eyes she went, clawing, his glasses, wrecked, on the floor —

You bitch, terrified, he screamed, I'll send you a fucking bill for the fucking glasses you fucking bitch I screamed. Protecting my eyes.

But she, on the bed, on the back, breasts hanging out, unspeakable grin on face. Then fucking take me take me take me you SHIT.

And he picked up the screwed-up glasses and he made to leave and she picked up her scissors used to cutting up stage sets and he didn't wait to see the close-up and he slammed the door behind him and then once out in the street he ran, despite the trembling he ran. Oh, love.

The heart was racing now, one continuous wall of sound,

impossible to count the beat. Clutching garden fences he made it home.

I've come home, mother, this is my home, mum, mummy, he cried to the empty space. Where is the feast, the suckling pig, the odour of spices, of caraway, of caraway above all, the mountain dumplings, the sauerkraut? Mumsy? And in the fridge half a can of baked beans. And in the freezer half a pack of chips. Culinary.

Oh no, I am not complaining, motherson outgrown, umbilical cord severed. It's just that she should be here, waiting, clean shirts ironed waiting, for the sailor son.

What? The Swimmer? Not yet.

Waves of fear, however, as streetlamps turn into monstrous moons, with the advancing night. And his own reflexion, in the window-pane, and the cateyes of a tower block. And the noises of the heater, imitating a break-in, through the wall. And the shadows of the weeping fig, shaken by Hades. And his own shadow, breaking free. And crumbtermites under feetsoles. And flyhornets under lampshades. And out in the street and in to the Off-licence and back with the brandy. And in with the brandy and listen to the chest thaw. And look at the one moon in the sky and smile at the cosy lamps. And admire the beauty of the tree, unwithered. And marvel at the shadows. At the softness. Oh yes stretch out even, feel the warmth of the fire on the soles of your feet. Wriggle on your bum let loose your limbs with your forehead touch your knees straighten up again throw back your head sigh. Smile. You'll pull through, baby.

No telling at all where she could be hiding. Or where she could be coming out of it. Anything from congressing in Italy to a head buried in the bosom of a bosom pal. Hurting, maybe. Nail biting. With a shabby hat over the eyes maybe soaked in some rain maybe hiding the tears. Or hiding the tears in some sun gazing at it. Laughing I doubt it. Or yes maybe at the oddness of the missing willie of her bosom pal's underbosom. Remembering perhaps other times when with the procreator she faked it. The pleasure in the sucking of it. Or did she ever suck the baseball bat she so often likened it to. Though I doubt that even He ever could compare. His tool I mean even in its greatest glory leading him down the stairs into her bedroom popping buttons. When she looked in horror and disgust upon it. When she had looked with admiration and a little fear upon it. Now laughing at the smallness of it. Now wishing for the baseball bat. Now when there is nothing there. Now when she has to stick a handle into the other's gaping hole. Sisterly openings. When the gentleness runs out, when the patience is exhausted when goddammit something has to be found to plug the emptiness. Or is she trying to let out something with that fucking handle, a child she can share, a child from mother's belly.

Then fall behind the back of your brain leaving the lights on.

Then in the morning at noon wake up phone the shop be ill. Be witty. Can't dust my poetry today Haila am ill. What?

Something I ate. Yap. Yap. Bye. Wipe the smile off your face take your head in your hands feel ill. Never lie. Shift your attention to your stomach. Clutch it. Then remember the head then groan with the pain then go to the mirror then press your forehead against the cool glass. Take a step backwards look at yourself look at the last of the muscles edging their way towards the elbows. Maybe when reached cushions developed it will be easier to ponder things behind desks covered in yellowing paper. Maybe then elbow-born Nirvana. Maybe then exposed bones pyramids to salvation. To scale. Light a cigarette cough a lung out. Look at the floor to find nothing. Hide your disappointment. Never lie.

He looked at the bottle of cognac. He went to the bathroom and turned on the tap of hot water. He went back to look at the bottle of cognac. He heard a key turn in the lock. He heard shivers running up and down his spine. He heard a sigh and he heard the door shut. He heard her heavy footsteps and he wondered if she'd learnt them from him. Together with the sighs. When afterwards he moaned his way back up the stairs, leading now the lifeless giant, legs apart.

Mother.

Oh for Christ's sake what are you doing here I've told you before I need my privacy I'll have to take your keys away from you if you do this again you have your place this is my place I come home tired when I come home tired I want to be alone for Christ's sake Kye don't do this again.

I was going to have a bath.

♦ ♦ ♦

He wished he could walk straight. Not that he swayed from curb to fence. But he wished he could feel he walked straight. Firm. Without effort. Without having to concentrate on having to put one foot in front of the other. He wished he could just walk like that, firm, without thinking about the walking, just being able to look at the world and smile at it or curse it, smell it or run past smells, hear it or plug his ears with the latest joyful negative. And he wished he could get drunk without thinking about tomorrow's bigger shakes, and he wished he could smoke through new elated lungs, ready for the soiling. And he wished he had a place where the broom would make a difference. To go to.

The application of things in order to make a difference. Like an aeroplane applied to a spire. To topple it. And to self-destruct. Against a dramatic sky of clouds and the setting sun. With pages from the tomes of a passenger's life scattering over the city. With the blood and the guts of the others for adornment. With the final demise the final signature dis-placed in mid-air. And floating just above it, the broom.

Kye walked pondering thus in the drizzle, friend down there swelling for no reason. Or was it the broom. As she handles it, a pearl necklace touching the erect nipples of her firm breasts. As naked she. Bends over.

Shit, a miserable day, the warmth of a fire too far away to bother. As she bends over it. As naked she. As the fire draws patterns over the young whore's arse. As she pokes it. As I, standing behind, with the broom.

And the fucking bus shelter is useless against the hori-zontal rain. As I stick the broom up her other hole and collect the moisture of the fruits of passion in the cup of my hand. And the bus will never come.

Then sitting on the upper deck trousers damp. Something functions.

Outside stale bread's rolling on the pavement. Kicked by a hungry tramp. By an angry hungry tramp. Bloody bastard can't convert it into beer. Suck on it you cunt in some hole where we can't see you. You stink you swine all the way up to the gallery. Passed now, a hangover of fury lingering. Force your mind to dwell on beauty's languor. On clean hot rocks by a clean blue sea in clean hot air with clean young bodies adorning the picture. Break through the roof of the bus to see this. With iron shaking shaking shaking fists. Lover.

Then out of the bus just before the zones change. Not up to crossing zones. In this weather. No more ascesis of the aspiring monk. Make your way through the endless drizzle. Not far to walk think of stepping stones in crystal clear brooks. While resting in the scaling of mountains. Think of the sprinkling of showers as the rapids hit the rocks. Think of your body being borne. Hello John.

Long time no see.

Oh friend.

May I offer you.

Yes indeed.

Then they sat down, sat there, friends. When tables still available. Round tables with heavy anchors reminiscent of steadier times and lighter heads. That they had never shared.

Yo, John.

Yo Kye.

Still trying to plough colours through the mud?

Aye.

And they sat there, and they talked of bricks. Red bricks, grey bricks, brown bricks. Bricks to chisel out of walls. Easier than sowing colours in the mud. Bud.

Dy. And he said to him buddy.

And he said to him Budweiser they don't serve here don't take the red and the white and the blue too seriously and especially not the stars.

Everything is fading.

The time will come when contrasts will sharpen.

Again?

In the meantime the smudge.

Oh boy let them not sharpen again.

Knives in the bellies?

Let them not.

Oh boy and there they were like yellowing like yellowed pages. Hiding from the howling wind. Peeking at the howling wind. From behind the glass.

How long do you think we have before the wind. Abates? But there they are sipping something to steady something else. Biding for time.

Will the temperature rise?

Before we have to go out?

Will it become? Dry?

Oh boy and there they were afraid of the wind and afraid of the rain and afraid of the howling and of the lashing of it.

This, John, is temporary.

A temporary.

Shelter.

Oh boy and they nearly stretched their hands out towards each other and they nearly embraced each other but they. Restrained themselves. But they looked into each other's eyes but they looked briefly and the tears they. Suppressed.

Hey, what is there to cry about?, one of them said.

What. She's probably drowned in the river of her own afloating.

Who?

The Beloved.

But what about the Swimmer?

Not yet.

Maybe you'd like to think of a red car.

I'd like to think of bricks. Of a thin wall of bricks. To knock down.

Easy obstacles.

For easy minds.

You know.

I know.

I know.

You know.

Oh boy and there they were knowing wishing they had a red car to get into get away with in. From the rain get away with in.

Why red, though, why, Kye?

Bricks. Red bricks.

Building then. Building then fast machines red machines brick machines.

With cranes.

With me at top with you at top with me at bottom safe-keeping with muscles and height just in case you fall.

Just in case I fall, John.

That would be nice.

Yes.

To build something.

Do you think there are. Stones in the river?

Sure, sure there are.

Under the mud?

Under? Under and above, peaking above it, like Olympus.

So you think when drowning when descending possibly pierced possibly punctured so as not to have to float back up disfigured?

Yes but that is after, after. But what about the Swimmer, to save, before.

Yes but I first have to. Catch him. Spot him. Beg him. Appease him. Swim towards him. In the ocean.

Bah.

In amongst the waves.

I have a little money set aside.

He is not to be bought.

To buy a little red car, and to fuck him.

He is not to be bought.

To get away in.

But she, then, unsaved, unblessed, unold, pierced by a rock.

Unwrinkled.

Young, still.

Dead young.

Young, still.

Yes.

But the Swimmer is coming.

I have a little money set aside.

Keep it, John, keep it. I must to the coast.

Don't.

To the coast indeed he would and with what and how and where to stay. And after all having just come back. I ask you. Having not met him. Not waited for him. Too scared to.

Not that I am scared John. Ny.

No of course not but still think of it.

Muscles certainly awesome.

To the good or to the bad?

But still he to save her.

Ah but proof.

Of good intent?

Just think of it.

A swimmer like that crossing oceans.

Have another.

What?

Drink.

Yes.

Just think of it and what if maybe when saved he.

Here.

Thanks I was just thinking maybe what if when he saves he.

Ah.

But he saves anyway if saved then hope.

Ah?

I drink this beer here with you John and it feels cool.

So forget it.

He forgot it he did kind of forget it Kye in the front of his mind.

Then the sentences started swimming. Then the Beloved was in the past, on a rosy beach, on a rosy end of day. With Kye able-bodied showing off his prowess in the waves. With her delicate lying there on the golden sand watching. Then he was the swimmer and no other was needed. Then on top of the foaming crushing weight he laughed. Then castles were promised, and the promises were to be kept. Then sand turned into stone. But here a pale blue steamer is ploughing its way through the mud.

So what of the betrayals of enthusiastic captains. Saving when the passenger should have all the glory. Of jumping overboard, of avoiding the whirling paddles. Hell but just too late, always just too late and the captain smiling putting on his white pristine hat with the shining badge conquering the sun. And the glory stays with the uniform and the world rests on golden epaulettes. The heart of the fair maiden, of course, is polishing the sailor's boots.

However, we do not grow strong with age, like trees. However. Our fatness is not majestic. And we do not cover ourselves with green at four times our limit. Ashes. Organic fertilizers for the ultimate greenness of others. So this is. A profoundness? What of the withering of black bodies in white deserts? Oases?

But this is masterly. Soiled pants hanging on a laundry line to dry, recently moistened. Potential ashes mixed with the moisture and the clay is ready for remodelling. So per-haps is the mud from the river. Mixed also with some sort of decay though not burnt. So time is perhaps after all on our side, on the clay's side. Even stones turn to it.

A little demonstration would be needed now, John, though I am too embarrassed to spit in the ashtray. Besides, the sign behind the bar says DO NOT. Still, what are red bricks made of.

Then the bell rang for the first time.

With clenched fists you know I thought I would go through life and with gritting teeth. When I tried to cover our traces in the snow. With purpose I would walk from life-post to life-post, stopping only to look up briefly at the sky to see my lucky star. Through cloud and rain I would see it up there, cold and sweaty with decision. And humourlessly, with absolute conviction, I would measure my steps. For the nation I would do it, for others I would do it, for the lumps of clay already forming in my reincarnate throat. Yes, those were the days when the sight of rotting leaves was a sign of Hope. When the thighs of women inspired Purity, when policemen's batons were pointers to salvation. And their fists. Digging my nails in the palms of my hands, line of mouth curving downwards, top of the head crushing the oncoming winds, I was going to live to win. Long hair flowing, let us not forget. And an old oversized coat belonging to father with a fox fur collar to add to the dash. For in spite of the clay-bound mission, style.

Then the bell rang for the second time.

But how long, I ask you, could the coat have remained

oversized when I, suddenly, shot up to overtake my neigh-
bours, in actual height? With my father shrinking in some
dark corner of his own making. Goddammit the seams would
have burst if I had tried to put it on. Leaving it behind, then,
along with the other paraphernalia of purpose. Along with
the clenched fists and the reverse smile. Along with the head-
butting position of the neck. Along with the locks of wavy
hair. And then, with flapping arms, with palms of hands
exposed to the elements, with face lashed by the wind and the
rain, I landed, here.

But what is this, as we stand outside, undecided, up there,
stars? With two lucky ones among them? Don't think that,
friend, don't look up, not even briefly. And undecided we go,
each our own way, and we look back, and we flap our arms.

Go while the going's good, somebody said, or something
like. Sure but in what direction that I hadn't tried before?
Said something about North and South, north to south.
Peckham? But I am going to catch the last train north, and I
am going to miss Kentish Town West, and I am going to get
off at Gospel Oak, and the rain will be pouring down, and
the stars will have disappeared, and I will be lost, and I will
be soaked through, and I am going to catch a taxi though I
could have walked if I hadn't been lost, and I am going to pay
a lot of money to the driver, and he is going to revile me for
having to take me such a short distance, and bloody foreign-
ers, and I will enter my hovel and Denise won't be there and
even the other stupid John won't be there, and she will have

drunk my whisky. Shit I sit on my bed mattress the room still stinks of piss other aromas blended to give it character thank God I'd bought a fresh packet of desert animals to smoke. But hell why when I need her most. When I need the whisky most and she in a nightclub on her way to one having poured my liquor into somebody else's coke bottle with pangs of conscience from time to time I know she thinks of me she'll buy me a bottle tomorrow I don't need it tomorrow I need it now. I sit restless on my bed mattress smoking a camel think suddenly what about that Greek Turkish restaurant cum illegal late night drunkards' haven just around the corner it's open till three four it's only twelve now. So yes I get up again put on shoes dry clothes now take somebody's umbrella in the hallway or is it mine have purchased such articles before. Briskly I walk with tongue still grown to the lower jaw only metaphorically hanging out. I turn round the corner almost head-butting with purpose passing a plush joint my joint is shut it being shut my joint shuts on Tuesdays. Clenching my fists now I curve the corners of my mouth to form a snarling half moon I lower my head I go back passing the plush joint still open I stop I turn on my heels I enter the plush joint two cops sitting at a table two pointers to salvation hanging from their hips two glasses of sin hovering between the thumb and index. To diffuse my situation I light an acceptable I approach the barman I buy two bottles of lukewarm retzina to take away strictly illegally the cops are having a good time what if I picked up a phone denounced them did something

for humanity had two humane drinking lazy cops sacked jeopardized for ever for some time this unique possibility of quenching frustration so late so late in this town I smile at the cops as I hide the bottles under my armpits I even wink at the cops they don't wink back I am out now I am running whizzing round the corner running through a shortcut past windows not yet playing Kylie Minogue playing that's it Jazz no not quite I find myself sprinting where is the trembling now not too far to go now a police siren behind me not for me skilfully I open and shut the door.

Rushing into my room opening and shutting the door what the hell unskilfully I land on the mattress hell with a thud the stuffing's bad coming out of the sides I put the bottles by my left hip I reach for the bottle opener by my left cheek impeccably the cork is screwed out it pops bottle to lips glass decorum hey we are in private. I stretch out my legs, I feel the thigh muscles unfold, I feel the hip bones digging in the bed. I recline my head, I make a dune in the cushion, I light a cigarette, I look at the ceiling, I blow smoke at the discoloured ceiling. I am glad Denise isn't here, I am glad the other stupid John isn't here. I talk to myself. I brace myself against the wind and the howling of it. I am not against anything or anyone. I half-lie half-sit in silence. Silence of others. I talk to myself. When the wind is this strong it is impossible to predict the outcome. What will or will not fall. Some things bend right to the ground then spring up again strengthened. Some trees do that. Others break. The poles of high-jumpers do that. Then they break. It's not with clenched fists that I say this on the contrary the palm of my right hand is open facing upwards in a gesture of trusting abandonment. My left hand is gently embracing the neck of the bottle. I am not violent. I lie here trustingly. I don't wait for anyone and I don't want anyone to wait for me. I am not my own master but I am my own consoler. Now even the rain has stopped. At least I can't hear it. Now only the persistence of the squatters' drumming from next door. I am relaxed now, I have my legs stretched out, my head is buried in the cushion, I am not hiding my face, my arms are limp in the hugging of my body, I am not clenching any-thing, I do not want to I do not need to squat. I half-lie I half-sit here. I talk to myself. The front door opens I hear it fly open hit the old piano in the hallway. But I wanted to lie down here in the quiet and talk to myself and hit the bottle or the two. Then Denise a man too laughing in the hallway Denise third whispering third shouting third laughing sh Kye might be asleep Lou. Hell maybe she's brought Lou Reed back with her wouldn't surprise me one bit. The black horse took the bit between his teeth and I was helpless hold-ing the reins squeezing the saddle with my knees just holding on praying for him to get tired. My thighs stiffened now I dug my nails in the palms of my hands I let go of the bottle I didn't make a sound. Maybe quietly they will but the pres-ence is enough to. Too late she's seen the light through the badly fitting door. Now she will knock on it. First she says

I bet Kye'll have some booze. He always does.
Quickly I hide the other bottle then jump back on the bed.
The knock comes.

Yeah?

It's me Denise, Kye, Can I come in?

Sure.

She opens the door just to fit her head in grins sweetly. I act annoyed.

I'm sorry about the whisky Kye.

Sure.

(Pause)

Dammit Denise you know how much I need it when I get back.

You know I'll give it back to you Kye.

Yes I know Denise but oh what the.

Listen I thought maybe.

You and Lou would like some booze.

Well only if.

The Greek's still open.

No the Turk's shut we've just been.

Oh Den.

Oh well I just thought maybe you'd like to smoke some shit.

You know I don't like it.

Come on relax man come on relax man come on up.

Where's Lou?

Lou's up.

Lou wasn't Reed. He was a designer skinhead with a lisp and a pattern on his skull. He sat sprawled on Denise's cushion on Denise's mattress on Denise's floor. It made me mad that he did that. He was sprawling there with a grin sprawling on his face. It made me mad that sprawling grin and the buckles of his bondage trousers unbuckled sprawling on the cushions.

Hi I'm Kye.

I said extending my hand to him not bending so the bastard'd have to sit up to reach it.

Hi I'm Lou.

he said not sitting up not reaching it just barely raising his manicured claws.

Who's this asshole

I said pointing to the asshole turning to Denise.

Oh Lou's alright

Denise said telling Lou to roll a joint sprawling down beside him.

When you get to know him.

I'm quite easy to get to know

Lou said.

I wanted to say something like I am not sure I want to make the effort or You bet asshole or git but instead I sat down on the floor Turkish style took a swig from the bottle passed it to Denise said nothing stared at the carpet.

Are you tired?

Denise said

Kye?

116

I was tired and I was pissed off and I wanted to but never mind but I said

No pass me the joint.

I like the guy

Lou said grinning passing me the joint.

Yeah he's alright is Kye

Denise said

When you get to know him.

I stuck the thing between the fore and the ring fingers of my right hand, cupped my hands together, and inhaled as much of the devil as I possibly could.

I like the guy

Lou said

I'm beginning to know him.

I was tough and I was strong and I could smoke and drink the guts off anyone. I Kye with the Beloved I don't give a fuck about.

I like the guy

Shut up Lou.

I sat there tough and strong not giving a fuck waiting for the joint.

Hey Denise

I said

Where've you been tonight.

I asked this taking the joint not listening to the answer. I saw the bloody window starting to move towards me, and I saw the ceiling starting to move down on top of me, and I saw the walls starting to shrink, and I knew it was just a stupid hashish trip, and I knew it was a bad trip, and I knew I was freaked out, and I couldn't move. And I didn't wish I was downstairs sitting on my bed mattress drinking my wine mindbody relaxed the quiet listening to my tears or to my anger or to my resignation. I was just concentrating with all my might to keep the ceiling from coming down on top of me, to keep the window-panes from cutting up my face. I hate you Lou.

Kye woke up with the centre of gravity wobbling in his bowels. Thrusts of pain like radar waves spreading out from below the bellybutton. It was his free day, his day of rest. Down in the would-be kitchen among the debris in a niche of dust a bag of stale bagels Denise had found the night before. They should be like that, Denise assured him, bagels, hard. Among recent acquisitions a kettle and a working fridge with somebody's margarine and milk. On a recently built shelf somebody's tea. Somebody's sugar. Sweeten your life. Release the flow of energy or at least the flow of something. Take up the hot seat in the cold bog hope it will flush. But the speed of life wasn't like that hurtling forward. It was more like a giant piece of wobbling jelly, a thousand tremors to make one step. To take one sip of the laxative, for that matter. Then shift back up again from wall to railing from palm to elbow with the trembling cup. With it half empty slump on the bed spill some more on your tee shirt as you slump on the bed. Then remove the hard margarine-covered saliva-dribbling circle of nourishment from your mouth and deposit it on the aromatic floorboards. Don't even look at it.

To recline on the large green cushion, a piece from home, a piece of mother. Having eaten a large evening meal. Having spent the day in mental and physical exertion. For a Cause. Blood flowing freely, limbs obeying every impulse of the spine. Adventure round every corner, or the possibility of it. White knights in front, black knights in back, course of direction clear. Shake the evil off your heels, heart always pure. Overwhelming driving force of love. The deep inhaling of it. The coupling of souls. And all the while the muscles tuned to play on. All the while Purpose.

Instead here.

Instead not over there in the hills of Moravia, for example, undulating. Walking with a specially crafted cane with a heavy rucksack on my back. With a wide-brimmed hat on my head. In the July sun. With a loving father and a loving mother and a beloved brother to a hidden cottage to faint for the first time deliciously watching the cut in my index finger. To fade beautifully away to come to beautifully again. To father's sneer and mother's laughter and brother's horror. To the family. Then to listen in awe to the evening storm. To the rain drumming on the wood. Then to the silence after. To seal the magic.

Then the hidden bottle remembered. Warm white wine in the morning contemplated. Then effort made to dress, to shiver down to the off-licence clutching garden fences to pay with a sweaty hand to face the contempt of the Indian seller to feel way back to the house to slump on the bed underskin underhead buzzing to crack open a can. To be bored of himself. To kneel on the bed face buried in cushion to fart to the ceiling. To make the inner and outer spaces into one equal stinking. To be extrovert.

part 2

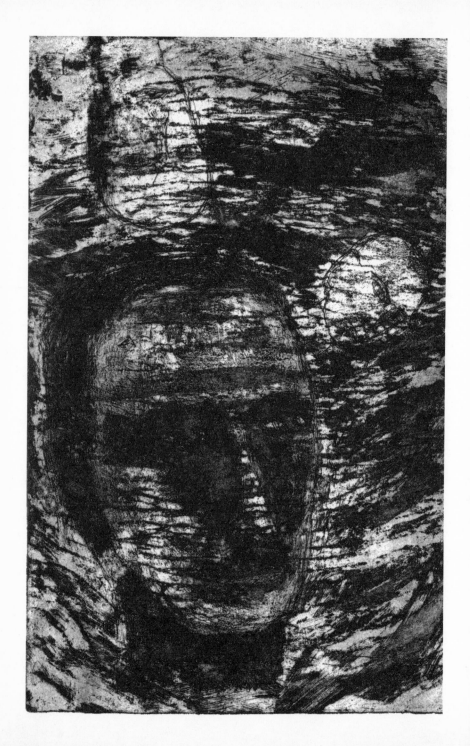

Diabolical the way he, broad-shouldered, beats the waves. White miners' hat on, torch shining. In the dark the torch, foam spuming forth around it. Hectic strength. Lone frantic domination of the element. Steady in the frant though, sure, like the shark. Never for a moment the drowning frant, the helpless engulfment. No, beating the water with vengeance, with superiority, using the water arrogantly as a foothold for his strength, spreading the pool of his strength out into it. Then his pool submerges the sea, and rests upon it, and tames it. Or rather, channels the wildness. Or rather gathers it, then spits it out. Like the sperm whale. Yes, with contemptuous playfulness. Spits the sea out. Spits out a challenge.

Challenge accepted by Kye in his heart and in his underbelly. Muscles, too, jerkily responding. To the bus stop he braves the shivers. To the Indian alcohol provider, first, for a flask. Then on the bus on the top deck sitting shivering staring out not seeing. Resolution mingled with the sweat now, set in the tight lips. Clutching the cold metal bar of the seat in front, visions of dark waters. Too shy to open the flask now, too shy to take a swig, too proud to show a weakness. Kye doesn't need crutches now, artificial stimuli. Kye is a man determined, now. Kye has courage. Even in the changing of buses, on the pavement, Kye stands freely — not firmly, no — not leaning against the bus shed. Back on the top deck of the other bus even the shivers seem to subside, with only the heart pounding. A healthy pounding of the heart, an adrenalin kind of pounding, a before a contest kind of pounding, before a challenge. Alighting at Victoria, making the bus lighter with the removal of his body, he shows firm resolve. Into the crowd he plunges, glad now to be thinking of dark waters. He progresses, shuffle by shuffle, to the parting of money in exchange for the right to a journey. Quite coolly now, with a trained eye, he surveys the queues, and picks the shortest. Out comes the wallet now, in readiness, in the bulging, the pay-day wallet. The person in front of him, whom he hadn't noticed until now, his mind on another, a mini-skirted creature of uncertain origins, legs glorious in the railway station sun, approaches the window. He loses himself for a moment, follows the legs as they, lithely, turn and walk away and on and later on to and into and later under or above somebody lucky and then he hears Sir! and he turns to the yellow sexless visage behind the glass and then he hears Kye! and he turns away again from the yellow visage and then he sees — Asde, and then he feels a poke in the ribs and then he knows his place in the queue is lost and then Asde where the hell have you sprung from and then the embraces and the hugs and the kisses on both cheeks.

Asde, where the hell have you sprung from? Asde's been to Germany, just for a while, just for a few days, to visit father and mistress, a family obligation, if you can call it that, a family, I mean. Could be her sister, the mistress, could be his daughter. Hates her. They hate each other, the daughter and the mistress. I would too I Kye if I had a brother like that.

And love?

Oh God don't talk to me about him.

Whom? Asde I've got a train to catch.

Where to? Paris?

I wish. Yes in a way via the sea.

Yes of course via the sea how else?

I have to swim across.

In this cold? Swim across in this cold?

Asde I've got a train to catch.

He looked over his shoulder at the queue the queue was long. He heard the announcer announce the immediate departure of his train. He heard Asde say what the hell Kye there'll be another one. He heard her say let's have a drink I've got so much to tell you. He felt his resolve dissolving.

Here? A drink?

Grim, I admit.

Where, then?

At my place. I've got a duty free spirit in my bag.

But Asde, I've made a resolution. I've got to go swimming.

Go swimming tomorrow.

But Asde, you don't understand, a friend is waiting for me, this very minute, in amongst the waves.

Kye?

Yap?

Let's take a taxi.

— ?

I'll pay.

In the taxi he felt a mixture of relief and guilt. Mixed in the mind, mixed in the heart, mixed in the underbelly. Then he felt her warmth, then he felt her fun, then he felt the bottle in her bag, then he began to melt, then he stretched his legs, then he crossed them at the ankles with the knees apart, then he pushed his left shoulder forward then the right, then he eased them into broadness, then he eased his jaw, then he closed his eyes, then he opened them, then he looked at her, then he smiled.

You bitch, he said.

She put the heating on, she put the kettle on, for tea, for the cold, she put the music on, he danced, for the warmth. She took the bottle out of the bag, he rinsed two glasses, she poured the stuff in. Hell why bother with the tea.

And then the conversation started rolling, like the umpteenth time seen Hollywood Monday afternoon TV movie. About inept customs officers, about English yobs in drunken stupor on the football boat, about lack of finesse, about never ever travelling by ferry again, about Germany's excessive propriety, about Germany's vulgarity in riches, about stupid parents, about all the same beloved parents, about an artist with a tasteful yacht on a lake, about London dirt, about London hate, about London love, about boyfriends, about loving dilemmas, about hairstyles, about the clothes of yobs, about the clothes of yuppies, about his taste, about the other's lack of it, about smoking too much, about what the hell, about being yourself, about having to write trash, about having to write, about wanting it, about wanting to be, something, other —

And all the while the Swimmer beating the waves down — And all the while he listened sipping the brandy not wanting to drink it drinking it feeling like a traitor thinking of the Swimmer beating the waves down feeling like a wimp.

And how the hell am I going to be strong enough tomorrow if I don't eat?

North American Indian four day fasting ordeal torture following then joining battle? But then the rest of the time healthy living. Pure air. Horseback.

He listened to her reluctantly, he didn't find her funny, he minded the mindlessness. He sat on the edge of his chair, he counted the seconds on the kitchen clock. Sixty to the minute, all right. False time. He switched his attention to her foot instead, jerking to the music. Not pretty, the jerking foot. Under other circumstances, of course. In a different time.

He didn't want to look her in the eyes. For fear of meeting empty sockets. Death-masks began to haunt him. Empty sockets. Then pockets, idiotically, suggested themselves to him. Pockets empty of what? Hands? Money? Pockets full of something? An erect cock switching sides? Oh but come now this late in the brandy hour? Is it the sea that does it?, the thought of a cold sea? Or the thought of a rotting beloved?

Oh Asde it's so late I'm sorry I'm so very tired can I crash out here on the carpet go to sleep catch my train in the morning? Please?

No.

You are joking.

No I'm not.

Oh come on.

No really Kye it's too small in here I need my privacy. Now if I had another room.

Please Asde I'll sleep under the desk over there be quiet as a mouse blind as its winged sister.

No you wouldn't you'd try to sleep with me.

No I wouldn't Kye was angry now.

Yes you would what's that growing in your trousers?

That's not because of you Kye recrossed his legs, that's because, it's because, of my beloved, rotting, in the river.

Kye you're foul.

Come on honey you can't expect me to go all the way back home? From where I started?

But why not it's almost equidistant to the station.

But it's the principle.

I don't have time for principles you should know that, Kye.

You are a real bitch, you know.

I know. She was smug, now.

You ARE joking.

Kye, and she looked at him very, very straight crossing her arms on her chest, I am not joking.

What do you expect me to do then, Kye was flustered now, get a cab? At this hour? With no money? Or walk? Ha?

You can wait for the first bus. You can sit here with me and you can talk to me and drink with me and then you can take the first bus.

He was very flustered then, for a minute, he felt like hitting her then, for a second but suddenly, like a prisoner resigned to his trap, he relaxed, leaned back, and emptied the hitherto sipped glass in one gulp. You are a bitch, you know.

I know. She was smug, then, also.

Strange that no feeling of anger. On the contrary, a positive feeling of friendship. Of admiration, even. He looked her in the eyes and, finding the sockets full, said, You are a bitch, you know. And you've got lovely green eyes.

 She smiled.

Before he left he counted the seconds one more time from twelve to twelve. Sixty. Five.

Back on the pavement back at a bus stop he examined the timetable for the arrival of the first bus. Six. He sat down on the steps property of the American Church (ditto), and began to count sixty times sixty.

When he reached home, the hole he called home the stinking pisshole when he climbed the stairs of the — front garden rubbish dump — as he — forced the bent key through the rusty keyhole, he thought Why, didn't I take the first morning bus, to the station? Why, in my imbecility, did I, come, back, here? Like a wind-up toy? Start from the beginning? Does everything have to restart all the time? From the dregs? Journeys? One step forward two steps behind? Pages scrapped start again from the virgin white? Why not just walk in a straight line from one end of death to the other. Why the zigzags. Growing your hair long then cutting it short. Having cut it short wishing it was long. Living in the hope. Living from hair to hair. Ach, mournful morns.

Make sense he did not or did he now did he. Would like to know a girl named Didi (dee-dee but shorter, the vowels, as in if but softer, softer). A little boyish, short hair anyway, a girl with hope, therefore, even the face a little boyish to go with the hair, small upturned nose, large doe's eyes, uncertain mouth. But down below the hollow of the neck, a porn-queen: large breasts, between which I'd, and then, down there, it, partly shaved, for worship, for magical entries, for ablutions, for burying precious objects in, for overblown seeds of the earth, for countless attempts at a return to before the rays of the doctor's lamp announced to my annoyed eyes the start of the death path. Then her backside, turning her over, spreading her legs, for punishment. For letting me out.

Ah, mournful morns. What to think of, in the endless twilight? Eh, romantic?

Friends?, yes of course one has friends.

One has enemies also, one hopes, enemies enough to care enough to kill one. Oh, to be killed by an enemy. In a duel. Over Didi. For Didi, only Didi is worth killing for. And she doesn't exist.

Ach, mournful morns, kneeling on the rotting mattress, itself lying on the rotting boards. Remembering the Beloved is painful, on such occasions. In such dirt. Recalling the purity, while staring at months of old stains on the rotting sheets. Unloving stains. Stains of frustration. Stains of rot. Ah, humour. Me, humour me, she would say, taking his hands into hers. Kiss me. But I couldn't now, love, I couldn't now even if you were here, even if you materialized, even if you sat here, right in front of me, naked, supple, calm, open, I couldn't now. For the rot in my mouth. For the sour decay. Oh please, forgive me. Shadows are playing on the wall, infecting my brain. Their game is not funny.

But where am I, where is he kneeling on this filth staring through filth at more of the same? Dreaming of a mythical journey through hell while lying in a Roman bath? God no this is real man I am in the bag with the rest of the rubbish. So to go to sleep on this in this? Even though God having had none or is that better? Still drunk? Isn't that better still drunk to hit the streets? Again? While still not shivering from soberness? While still posing questions?

So up he stood. Took out a cigarette lit it. Tastes good. Out the door breathing the smoke in not breathing the air in. To take the second morning bus into town. To the station. To the sea. But then suddenly he stood irresolute. For a moment he even contemplated going back to sleep in the garbage room. Shuddered at the thought. No. Took a step forward. In the middle of the pavement now, looking left, looking right. Rightward the bus. Leftward the overground train. To Mother's. Would she be in? If not, he could sleep there, in his brother's room. He could spread out. He could rest. He could eat, even, perhaps. Regain his strength. Leftward. Yes.

On the train he reproached himself with cowardice. He should have taken the bus. He should have gone for it. He should have had faith. He should have gone. He was late as it was. The Swimmer was waiting. The Beloved was to be saved. But he just wasn't in the right frame of mind. Or body. He needed refreshment. He needed to be strong. To swim in the cold sea. Surely, the Swimmer, would understand that. The train, rattling away, the local train. From hole to Mother. Fear.

Fearfully he unlocked the front door. Stopped. Listened. Mother?, quietly. Mother?, louder. MOTHER! Up the steps he crept, not yet confident. He opened all the doors of all the three rooms. Motherless. He sighed. Relief mixed with disappointment. In a way he would have liked to, but never mind. Motherboy motherless. He would like her to give him strength again, like she used to. To give him understanding. He would like her to open up to him, and listen, and nod her head, and smile. He would like to hear her say that he was alright, that he's got what it takes, that he'll make it. He would like her to be there, ten years ago.

But in the fridge an opened tin of beans.

It's rotting here, too. With a worse rot, with the rot of an unstoppable human decomposition. With hope gone for ever with the first can of beans eaten cold. In one sitting. In front of J.R. He fishes in the dirty puddle in the dirty sink for a dirty mug, no tea. He sits down on a plastic stool with the seat half burnt, knees tight together. With hands tight together in between thighs. Staring for a moment not seeing numb. Images for a moment projected on inside of skull of another kitchen in another flat. Warmth as everybody's laughing or cursing living the father the mother the brother. Wanting to feed themselves. Wanting to be. He focuses again on the dirty floor leading to the dirty hallway leading to the dirty stairs, leading out. He is out.

Back in the street the shivers catch up with him. He's got to walk it through. He'll have a hamburger at the Head. He'll get strong. Or a pork chop. He should feel sleepy but the trembling has taken over. The trembling doesn't allow for sleep. He's got to walk this through. He tries not to lean on garden fences. He concentrates. Left foot, right foot. He's managing. You'll manage, a friend back there used to tell him, you will always manage. I mean look at you, with parents like that, with a mother like that, with genetics. I mean yeah, his sweaty hand clutches the cold metal of a garden fence. He steadies himself. Come on now, balance, legs wide apart, a sailor, a cowboy, a sharp shooter, one foot, then the other, walk. The hands, the legs, tingling. Not painfully. Like the wood of a guitar, after a loud chord. His face contorted with the effort of the mind to control. The casket. Any foreign thought and the whole thing falls apart. The hand flies to grip a metal bar. Every time the knees, tight together, need more pursuading, to bend. The feet again, to outdo each other. O.K. the pavement, square by square, to conquer. But then, too much emphasis on the immediate below, all his weight shifts to the head and again, doubled up, he squeezes the metal bar at its root now, embedded in the concrete. O.K., a broader field of vision necessary, or rather the bulls-eye of a moving target, let's say the run on that girl's stockings, just the right distance in front. Yes, semi-stability is achieved, walking in the middle of the pavement now. Highbury Corner. Too many points of focus. Girl lost in multitude. Confusion. No garden fences. O.K., switching from one target to the next, zigzag. Point de repère. At last, on the left the church, on the right the pub. A warm feeling of success floods over him, face relaxes a little. Inside, a couple of drunkards at the bar, a couple of couples at a couple of tables. It's quiet. He can hear his chest roar. Wonders if the others can hear. Indifference. He will have a drink now. He can't think of food now, he can't think of any-thing solid trying to fight its way down inside of him. He pictures inner scratches, inner bleeding. He stumbles to the bar. He orders a pint. He needs both hands to carry it to a table. He puts it down carefully, sits down, bends to take the first sip. Then with both hands, still bent, brings it to his lips, tilts it, drinks. Feels the quiet. Feels the liquid cushion his lungs. Looks up. Relaxes shoulders. Leans back. Smiles. The barmaid smiles, he notices her, he recognizes her, he winks at her, her smile broadens. Hey, Kye. He takes the pint with one hand, raises it in the air, in her direction, lets it hover there majestically for a while, then brings it to his lips, gulps the stuff down. Hey Kye. He feels strong now, but not strong enough to talk. He gestures towards his skull, apologetically. She understands. She understands his need for privacy. She is an actress. And a playwright. After all. They both look away, he at his glass, she just away, the way barmaids do. Contentment settles in, towards the end of the first drink. At the beginning of the second, courage. Not for any kind of action though, this courage. It's a courage for staying put, for lifting heavy liquids up to sore lips. Not for swimming. Nor for eating in order to swim. Not even for taking a bus to take a train to recover on a shore. No time, at any rate, for any recovery. This is I speaking though, not Kye. Kye feels muscles growing under his shirt, shoulders broaden, thighs stiffen. Kye doesn't need food. Kye defies nature. Kye is a spiritual being. And it only takes spirits to fuel his kind. God does he feel like Him he does. All-powerful. Who needs the Swimmer Kye certainly doesn't the Swimmer's just a poor sucker. Waiting there in the waves. Waiting for Kye. As if Kye needed him. As if he, Kye, needed a sucker. Like that. To save the Beloved. Maybe it's the other way round. Maybe the Swimmer needs Kye. To get at Beloved. Maybe that's been the Swimmer's plan all along. To use Kye. To get at Beloved. Yes, that must be it, how could Kye have been so blind? Kye can swim, Kye can swim it all the way. So who needs the

Swimmer? Let the sucker wait. Let the bloody scheming wimpo drown. Kye can swim, Kye can swim it all the way. He's got the motivation. He's got Love to save. And the seams of his shirt can hardly contain the eager, bulging biceps. His pants have become too tight for his enormous thigh muscles, he has to stretch his legs right out, like a sailor, to ease the pressure. He can sense, he can see the admiring uneasy glances of the public, for he has taken centre stage, not daring to look at him for long, afraid of his wrath. He is riding high. And soon, soon, he will get up, and walk out of here, into the unknown. He will not look back. Soon, but not just yet. He is in no hurry. Beloved's dead, anyway. Stuck under a stone somewhere in the Seine. Waiting for a breath of life. And if she's in a river, why the fuck do I have to swim across the fucking sea? Yet there somehow his reasoning failed him. It was somehow necessary to swim across the fucking sea. Like it is necessary to walk to Compostella, not take a bus. Like it was necessary for Herzog to walk from Munich to Paris to save Lotte Eisner, not take a bus. Like a pilgrimage. But the thought of a pilgrimage made him feel weak. The dependence on higher powers. The supplication. God. The Swimmer. Sobriety. Triple scotch. And what if Beloved, somewhere on the surface, a floating purple balloon? Resurrecting that? Giving that the kiss of life? Piercing it perhaps with a pin listening to the hissing smelling the gases? Accumulated? Not pretty. Madness perhaps surely to try to bring back the dead. Should

137

be left in peace surely, should live in our memories and dreams. But bloated on dirty waters? Peace? Too poisonous even for fish and gulls to peck at? Christ at least under the earth the worms do their job unseen. And what's this business about dreams and memories. I want her to touch me, alive. I don't want to think about even nicely hidden rotting flesh. Maggots. Dreams and memories. Kye felt the momentary weakness pass. Man is to be overcome. Fag after fag. Lungs singing in the spirit. John should be here. I wish John was here. John is strong. And calm. He'd even go down to the sea with me, if he could, if he had the time. See me off. Or Denise. She'd hold my hand. Like a friend. Like the friend she is. I don't have many friends. I had a lot, of friends. Back there. In the common cause. Fighting the tyrant. Or did I? Or friend, the definition of? Member of a pack? Or one to one, outside tribes. The latter, I think, the holding of hands in a limbo. But neither John nor Denise are here. Solitude overwhelms Kye. It is a solitary relationship, one and one's beloved. Not like friendship. Not like one and one, but a blending, into one. Not like building a red brick wall, Johnny, with me at top and you at bottom, ready to catch me should I fall. No, together there at bottom, crooked movements with crooked results. After the blending's been broken, that is, after first love. After the sleeping bag, so ample at first, becomes too small for two. But God damn it what am I talking about, the future? Let her sleep. If only I knew she was somewhere where she could be left to sleep. How I loved her when she was asleep, how I loved her then. I strong watching over her. Matched heart-beat to heart-beat. But her heart beat, Christ. Her heart BEAT. She was asleep, she was alive, she would wake. I want her awake.

Kye looked towards the door for Johnny or his ghost. Neither was there. He will have to reinvent them. Denise never comes here any more.

Trouble was John was real. Hard to play with. So was Denise.

But Kye needed help. Kye was beginning to feel afraid again, Kye needed a friend. To lean against. The hand was trembling again, with the half-a-glass to heavy to lift to lips. Too late for food now, to thicken the thinning muscles. Food bar's shut. And anyway. Kye's pure spirit. No need for. Body tricks.

Jeans flapping round the sticks of thigh-bones. Shoulder pads of jacket down to elbows. Neck too weak to support the heavy head. A little puddle of beer now the focus of vision. Maybe it is the sea.

London: 1989–1991

Kye by Lukáš Tomin / artwork by Alf Van der Plank / design by Chaim / set in Janson / first edition October 1997 / published by Twisted Spoon Press, P.O. Box 21—Preslova 12, 150 21 Prague 5, Czech Republic, e-mail: twispoon@terminal.cz / printed by Tiskárny Havlíčkův Brod / © at the front means that all rights are reserved under relevant laws and conventions, national, international, or otherwise; no reproduction of any part may be made without the permission of the publisher. / We thank: Louis Armand, Kip Bauersfeld, Kevin Blahut, Michaela Hajková, Amy Nestor, Marek Tomin, The Globe Bookstore, The Jáma Culture Foundation, The Terminal Bar, and Studio Forma

ISBN 80-901257-8-6